CONAN DOYLE
CENTENNIAL SERIES

OTHER NOVELS IN THE
CONAN DOYLE CENTENNIAL SERIES

The Mystery of Cloomber (1889)
The Firm of Girdlestone (1890)
The Doings of Raffles Haw (1892)
The Parasite (1894)
The Stark Munro Letters (1895)
The Tragedy of the Korosko (1898)
A Duet (1899)

Yours very truly
A Conan Doyle

Beyond the City

The Idyll of a Suburb

A. Conan Doyle

Afterword by Howard Lachtman

Illustrated by Pamela Mattix

GASLIGHT
PUBLICATIONS

BLOOMINGTON, INDIANA 1982

Beyond the City
was originally published in 1892
by George Newnes, Ltd., London

ISBN: 0-934468-44-3

Library of Congress
Catalogue Card No. 80-67703

Printed in the United States of America

First printing: April 1982

GASLIGHT PUBLICATIONS
112 East Second
Bloomington, Indiana 47401

Contents

List of Illustrations

BEYOND THE CITY

"Take care, Monica dear; don't let them see us."

1
The New-Comers

"If you please, mum," said the voice of a domestic from somewhere round the angle of the door, "number three is moving in."

Two little old ladies, who were sitting at either side of a table, sprang to their feet with ejaculations of interest, and rushed to the window of the sitting-room.

"Take care, Monica dear," said one, shrouding herself in the lace curtain; "don't let them see us."

"No, no, Bertha. We must not give them reason to say that their neighbours are inquisitive. But I think that we are safe if we stand like this."

The open window looked out upon a sloping lawn, well trimmed and pleasant, with fuzzy rosebushes and a star-shaped bed of sweet-william. It was bounded by a low wooden fence, which screened it off from a broad, modern, new metalled road. At the other side of this road were three large detached deep-bodied villas with peaky eaves and small wooden balconies, each standing in its own little square of grass and of flowers. All three were equally new, but numbers one and two were curtained and sedate, with a human, sociable look to them; while number three, with yawning door and unkempt garden, had apparently only just received its furniture and made itself ready for its occupants. A four-wheeler had driven up to the gate, and it was at this that the old ladies, peeping out bird-like from behind their curtains, directed an eager and questioning gaze.

The cabman had descended, and the passengers within were handing out the articles which they desired him to carry up to the house. He stood red-faced and blinking, with his crooked arms outstretched, while a male hand, protruding from the window, kept piling up upon him a series of articles the sight of which filled the curious old ladies with bewilderment.

"My goodness me!" cried Monica, the smaller, the drier, and the more wizened of the pair. "What do you call that, Bertha? It looks to me like four batter puddings."

"Those are what young men box each other with," said Bertha, with a conscious air of superior worldly knowledge.

"And those?"

Two great bottle-shaped pieces of yellow shining wood had been heaped upon the cabman.

"Oh, I don't know what those are," confessed Bertha. Indian clubs had never before obtruded themselves upon her peaceful and very feminine existence.

These mysterious articles were followed, however, by others which were more within their range of comprehension—by a pair of dumb-bells, a purple cricket-bag, a set of golf clubs, and a tennis racket. Finally, when the cabman, all top-heavy and bristling, had staggered off up the garden path, there emerged in a very leisurely way from the cab a big, powerfully built young man, with a bull pup under one arm and a pink sporting paper in his hand. The paper he crammed into the pocket of his light yellow dust-coat, and extended his hand as if to assist some one else from the vehicle.

To the surprise of the two old ladies, however, the only thing which his open palm received was a violent slap, and a tall lady bounded unassisted out of the cab. With a regal wave she motioned the young man towards the door, and then with one hand upon her hip she stood in a careless, lounging attitude by the gate, kicking her toe against the wall and listlessly awaiting the return of the driver.

As she turned slowly round, and the sunshine struck upon her face, the two watchers were amazed to see that this very active and energetic lady was far from being in her first youth, so far that she had certainly come of age again since she first passed that landmark in life's journey. Her finely chiseled, clean-cut face, with something red Indian about the firm mouth and strongly marked cheek bones, showed even at that distance traces of the friction of the passing years. And yet she was very handsome. Her features were as firm in repose as those of a Greek bust, and her great dark eyes were arched over by two brows so black, so thick, and so delicately curved, that the eye turned away from the harsher details of the face to marvel at their grace and strength. Her figure, too, was straight as a dart, a little portly, perhaps, but curving into magnificent outlines, which were half accentuated by the strange costume which she wore. Her hair, black but plentifully shot with grey, was brushed plainly back from her high forehead, and was gathered under a small round felt hat, like that of a man, with one sprig of feather in the band as a concession to her sex. A double-breasted jacket of some dark frieze-like material fitted closely to her figure, while her straight blue skirt, untrimmed and ungathered, was cut so short that the lower curve of her finely-turned legs was plainly visible beneath it, terminating in a pair of broad, flat, low-heeled and square-toed shoes. Such was the lady who lounged at the gate of number three, under the curious eyes of her two opposite neighbours.

But if her conduct and appearance had already somewhat jarred upon their limited and precise sense of the fitness of things, what were they to think of the next little act in this *tableau vivant?* The cabman, red and heavy-jowled, had come back from his labours, and held out his hand for his fare. The lady passed him a coin, there was a moment of mumbling and gesticulating, and suddenly she had him with both hands by the red cravat which girt his neck, and was shaking him as a terrier would a rat. Right across the pavement she thrust him, and, pushing him up against the wheel, she banged his head three several times against the side of his own vehicle.

"Can I be of any use to you, aunt?" asked the large youth, framing himself in the open doorway.

"Not the slightest," panted the enraged lady. "There, you low blackguard, that will teach you to be impertinent to a lady."

The cabman looked helplessly about him with a bewildered, questioning gaze, as one to whom alone of all men this unheard-of and extraordinary thing had happened. Then, rubbing his head, he mounted slowly on to the box, and drove away with an uptossed hand appealing to the universe. The lady smoothed down her dress, pushed back her hair under her little felt hat, and strode in through the hall-door, which was closed behind her. As with a whisk her short skirts vanished into the darkness, the two spectators—Miss Bertha and Miss Monica Williams—sat looking at each other in speechless amazement. For fifty years they had peeped through that little window and across that trim garden, but never yet had such a sight as this come to confound them.

"I wish," said Monica at last, "that we had kept the field."

"I am sure I wish we had," answered her sister.

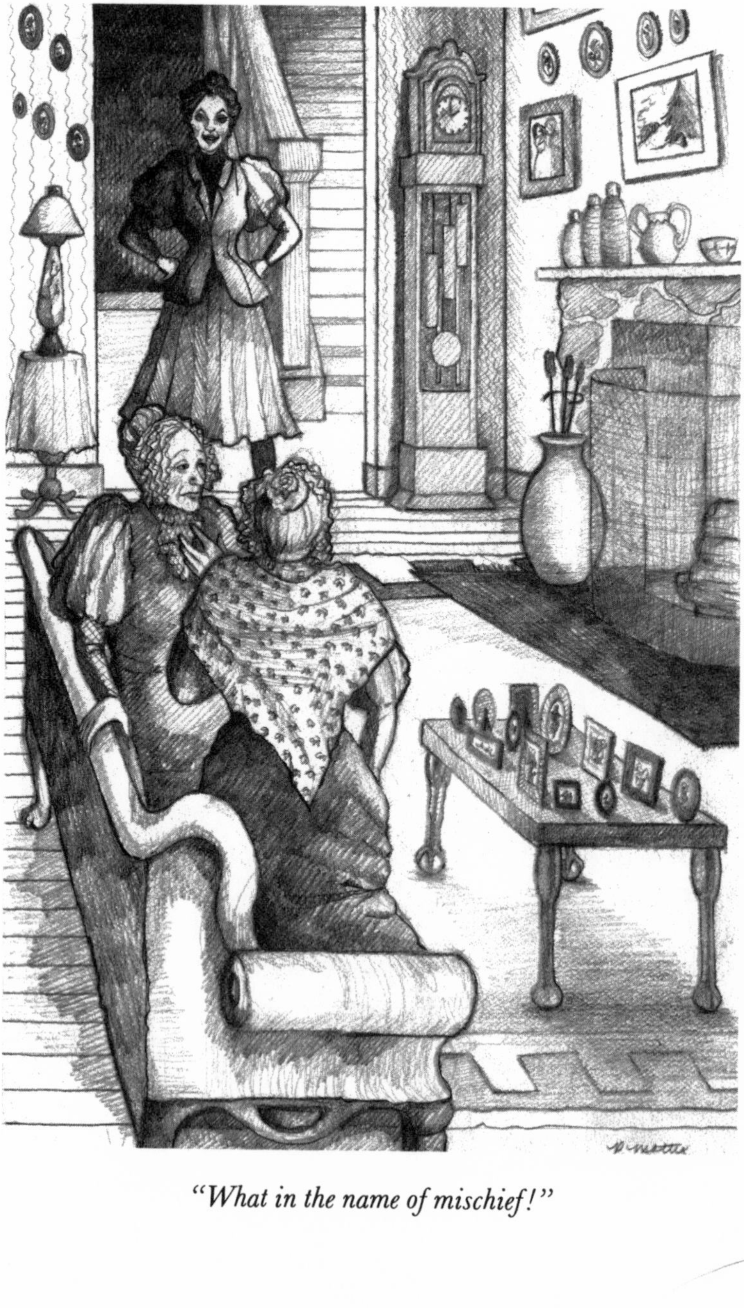

"What in the name of mischief!"

2
Breaking the Ice

THE COTTAGE from the window of which the Misses Williams had looked out stands, and has stood for many a year, in that pleasant suburban district which lies between Norwood, Anerley, and Forest Hill. Long before there had been a thought of a township there, when the Metropolis was still quite a distant thing, old Mr. Williams had inhabited "The Brambles," as the little house was called, and had owned all the fields about it. Six or eight such cottages scattered over a rolling country-side were all the houses to be found there in the days when the century was young. From afar, when the breeze came from the north, the dull, low roar of the city might be heard, like the breaking of the tide of life, while along the horizon might be seen the dim curtain of smoke, the grim spray which that tide threw up. Gradually, however, as the years passed, the City had thrown out a long brick-feeler here and there, curving, extending, and coalescing, until at last the little cottages had been gripped round by these red tentacles, and had been absorbed to make room for the modern villa. Field by field the estate of old Mr. Williams had been sold to the speculative builder, and had borne rich crops of snug suburban dwellings, arranged in curving crescents and tree-lined avenues. The father had passed away before his cottage was entirely bricked round, but his two daughters, to whom the property had descended, lived to see the last vestige of country taken from them. For years they had clung to the one field which faced their windows, and it was only after much argument and many heartburnings, that they had at last consented that it should share the fate of the others. A broad road was driven through their quiet domain, the quarter was re-named "The Wilderness," and three square, staring, uncompromising villas began to sprout up on the other side. With sore hearts, the two shy little old maids watched their steady progress, and speculated as to what fashion of neighbours chance would bring into the little nook which had always been their own.

And at last they were all three finished. Wooden balconies and overhanging eaves had been added to them, so that, in the language of the advertisement, there were vacant three eligible Swiss-built villas, with sixteen rooms, no basement, electric bells, hot and cold water, and every modern convenience, including a common tennis lawn, to be let at £100 a year, or £1,500 purchase. So tempting an offer did not long remain open. Within a few weeks the card had vanished from number one, and it was known that Admiral Hay Denver, V.C., C.B., with Mrs. Hay Denver and their only son, were about to move into it. The news brought peace to the hearts of the Williams sisters. They had lived with a settled conviction that some wild impossible colony, some shouting, singing family of madcaps, would break in upon their peace. This establishment at least was irreproachable. A reference to *Men of the Time* showed them that Admiral Hay Denver was a most distinguished officer, who had begun his active career at Bomarsund, and had ended it at Alexandria, having managed between these two episodes to see as much service as any man of his years. From the Taku Forts and the *Shannon* brigade, to dhow-harrying off Zanzibar, there was no variety of naval work which did not appear in his record; while the Victoria Cross, and the Albert Medal for saving life, vouched for it that in peace as in war his courage was still of the same true temper. Clearly a very eligible neighbour this, the more so as they had been confidentially assured by the estate agent that Mr. Harold Denver, the son, was a most quiet young gentleman, and that he was busy from morning to night on the Stock Exchange.

The Hay Denvers had hardly moved in before number two also struck its placard, and again the ladies found that they had no reason to be discontented with their neighbours. Doctor Balthazar Walker was a very well-known name in the medical world. Did not his qualifications, his membership, and the record of his writings fill a long half-column in the *Medical Directory,* from his first little paper on the "Gouty Diathesis" in 1859 to his exhaustive treatise upon "Affections of the Vaso-Motor System" in 1884? A successful medical career which promised to end in a presidentship of a college and a baronetcy, had been cut short by his sudden inheritance of a considerable sum from a grateful patient, which had rendered him independent for life, and had enabled him to turn his attention to the more scientific part of his profession, which had always had a greater charm for him than its more practical and commercial aspect. To this end he had given up his house in Weymouth Street, and had taken this opportunity of moving himself, his scientific instruments, and his two charming daughters (he had been a widower for some years) into the more peaceful atmosphere of Norwood.

There was thus but one villa unoccupied, and it was no wonder that the two maiden ladies watched with a keen interest, which deepened into a dire apprehension, the curious incidents which heralded the coming of the new tenants. They had already learned from the agent that the family consisted of two only, Mrs. Westmacott, a widow, and her nephew, Charles Westmacott. How simple and how select it had sounded! Who could have foreseen from it these fearful portents which seemed to threaten violence and discord among the dwellers in The Wilderness? Again the two old maids cried in heartfelt chorus that they wished they had not sold their field.

"Well, at least, Monica," remarked Bertha, as they sat over their teacups that afternoon, "however strange these people may be, it is our duty to be as polite to them as to the others."

"Most certainly," acquiesced her sister.

"Since we have called upon Mrs. Hay Denver and upon the Misses Walker, we must call upon this Mrs. Westmacott also."

"Certainly, dear. As long as they are living upon our land I feel as if they were in a sense our guests, and that it is our duty to welcome them."

"Then we shall call to-morrow," said Bertha, with decision.

"Yes, dear, we shall. But, oh, I wish it was over!"

At four o'clock on the next day, the two maiden ladies set off upon their hospitable errand. In their stiff, crackling dresses of black silk, with jet-bespangled jackets, and little rows of cylindrical grey curls drooping down on either side of their black bonnets, they looked like two old fashion plates which had wandered off into the wrong decade. Half curious and half fearful, they knocked at the door of number three, which was instantly opened by a red-headed page-boy.

Yes, Mrs. Westmacott was at home. He ushered them into the front room, furnished as a drawing-room, where in spite of the fine spring weather a large fire was burning in the grate. The boy took their cards, and then, as they sat down together upon a settee, he set their nerves in a thrill by darting behind a curtain with a shrill cry, and prodding at something with his foot. The bull pup which they had seen upon the day before bolted from its hiding-place, and scuttled snarling from the room.

"It wants to get at Eliza," said the youth, in a confidential whisper. "Master says she would give him more'n he brought." He smiled affably at the two little stiff black figures, and departed in search of his mistress.

"What—what did he say?" gasped Bertha.

"Something about a— Oh, goodness gracious! Oh, help, help, help, help, help!" The two sisters had bounded on to the settee, and stood there with staring eyes and skirts gathered in, while they filled the whole house with their yells. Out of a high wicker-work basket which stood by the fire there had risen a flat diamond-shaped head with wicked green eyes which came flickering upwards, waving gently from side to side, until a foot or more of glossy neck was visible. Slowly the vicious head came floating up, while at every oscillation a fresh burst of shrieks came from the settee.

"What in the name of mischief!" cried a voice, and there was the mistress of the house standing in the doorway. Her gaze at first had merely taken in the fact that two strangers were standing screaming upon her red plush sofa. A glance at the fireplace, however, showed her the cause of the terror, and she burst into a hearty fit of laughter.

"Charley," she shouted, "here's Eliza misbehaving again."

"I'll settle her," answered a masculine voice, and the young man dashed into the room. He had a brown horse-cloth in his hand, which he threw over the basket, making it fast with a piece of twine so as to effectually imprison its inmate, while his aunt ran across to reassure her visitors.

"It is only a rock snake," she explained.

"Oh, Bertha!" "Oh, Monica!" gasped the poor exhausted gentlewomen.

"She's hatching out some eggs. That is why we have the fire. Eliza always does better when she is warm. She is a sweet, gentle creature, but no doubt she thought that you had designs upon her eggs. I suppose that you did not touch any of them?"

"Oh, let us get away, Bertha!" cried Monica, with her thin, black-gloved hands thrown forwards in abhorrence.

"Not away, but into the next room," said Mrs. Westmacott, with the air of one whose word was law. "This way, if you please! It is less warm here." She led the way into a very handsomely appointed library, with three great cases of books, and upon the fourth side a long yellow table littered over with papers and scientific instruments. "Sit here, and you, there," she continued. "That is right. Now let me see, which of you is Miss Williams, and which Miss Bertha Williams?"

"I am Miss Williams," said Monica, still palpitating,

and glancing furtively about in dread of some new horror.

"And you live, as I understand, over at the pretty little cottage. It is very nice of you to call so early. I don't suppose that we shall get on, but still the intention is equally good." She crossed her legs and leaned her back against the marble mantelpiece.

"We thought that perhaps we might be of some assistance," said Bertha, timidly. "If there is anything which we could do to make you feel more at home——"

"Oh, thank you, I am too old a traveller to feel anything but at home wherever I go. I've just come back from a few months in the Marquesas Islands, where I had a very pleasant visit. That was where I got Eliza. In many respects the Marquesas Islands now lead the world."

"Dear me!" ejaculated Miss Williams. "In what respect?"

"In the relation of the sexes. They have worked out the great problem upon their own lines, and their isolated geographical position has helped them to come to a conclusion of their own. The woman there is, as she should be, in every way the absolute equal of the male. Come in, Charles, and sit down. Is Eliza all right?"

"All right, aunt."

"These are our neighbours, the Misses Williams. Perhaps they will have some stout. You might bring in a couple of bottles, Charles."

"No, no, thank you! None for us!" cried her two visitors, earnestly.

"No? I am sorry that I have no tea to offer you. I look upon the subserviency of woman as largely due to her abandoning nutritious drinks and invigorating exercises to the male. I do neither." She picked up a pair of fifteen-pound dumb-bells from beside the fireplace and swung them lightly about her head. "You see what may be done on stout," said she.

"But don't you think," the elder Miss Williams suggested timidly, "don't you think, Mrs. Westmacott, that woman has a mission of her own?"

The lady of the house dropped her dumb-bells with a crash upon the floor.

"The old cant!" she cried. "The old shibboleth! What is this mission which is reserved for woman? All that is humble, that is mean, that is soul-killing, that is so contemptible and so ill-paid that none other will touch it. All that is woman's mission. And who imposed these limitations upon her? Who cooped her up within this narrow sphere? Was it Providence? Was it nature? No, it was the arch enemy. It was man."

"Oh, I say, auntie!" drawled her nephew.

"It was man, Charles. It was you and your fellows. I say that woman is a colossal monument to the selfishness of man. What is all this boasted chivalry—these fine words and vague phrases? Where is it when we wish to put it to the test? Man in the abstract will do anything to help a woman. Of course. How does it work when his pocket is touched? Where is his chivalry then? Will the doctors help her to qualify? will the lawyers help her to be called to the bar? will the clergy tolerate her in the Church? Oh, it is close your ranks then and refer poor woman to her mission! Her mission! To be thankful for coppers and not to interfere with the men while they grabble for gold, like swine round a trough, that is man's reading of the mission of women. You may sit there and sneer, Charles, while you look upon your victim, but you know that it is truth, every word of it."

Terrified as they were by this sudden torrent of words, the two gentlewomen could not but smile at the sight of the fiery, domineering victim and the big apologetic representative of mankind who sat meekly bearing all the sins of his sex. The lady struck a match, whipped a cigarette from a case upon the mantelpiece, and began to draw the smoke into her lungs.

"I find it very soothing when my nerves are at all ruffled," she explained. "You don't smoke? Ah, you miss one of the purest of pleasures—one of the few pleasures which are without a reaction."

Miss Williams smoothed out her silken lap.

"It is a pleasure," she said, with some approach to self-assertion, "which Bertha and I are rather too old-fashioned to enjoy."

"No doubt. It would probably make you very ill if you attempted it. By the way, I hope that you will come to some of our Guild meetings. I shall see that tickets are sent you."

"Your Guild?"

"It is not yet formed, but I shall lose no time in forming a committee. It is my habit to establish a branch of the Emancipation Guild wherever I go. There is a Mrs. Sanderson in Anerley who is already one of the emancipated, so that I have a nucleus. It is only by organized resistance, Miss Williams, that we can hope to hold our own against the selfish sex. Must you go, then?"

"Yes, we have one or two other visits to pay," said the elder sister. "You will, I am sure, excuse us. I hope that you will find Norwood a pleasant residence."

"All places are to me simply a battle-field," she answered, gripping first one and then the other with a grip which crumpled up their little thin fingers. "The days for work and healthful exercise, the evenings to Browning and high discourse, eh, Charles? Good-bye!" She came to the door with them, and as they glanced back they saw her still standing there with the yellow bull pup cuddled up under one forearm, and the thin blue reek of her cigarette ascending from her lips.

"Oh, what a dreadful, dreadful woman!" whispered sister Bertha, as they hurried down the street. "Thank goodness that it is over."

"But she'll return the visit," answered the other. "I think that we had better tell Mary that we are not at home."

3
Dwellers in the Wilderness

HOW DEEPLY are our destinies influenced by the most trifling causes! Had the unknown builder who erected and owned these new villas contented himself by simply building each within its own grounds, it is probable that these three small groups of people would have remained hardly conscious of each other's existence, and that there would have been no opportunity for that action and reaction which is here set forth. But there was a common link to bind them together. To single himself out from all other Norwood builders the landlord had devised and laid out a common lawn tennis ground, which stretched behind the houses with taut-stretched net, green close-cropped sward, and widespread whitewashed lines. Hither in search of that hard exercise which is as necessary as air or food to the English temperament, came young Hay Denver when released from the toil of the City; hither, too, came Dr. Walker and his two fair daughters, Clara and Ida, and hither also, champions of the lawn, came the short-skirted, muscular widow and her athletic nephew. Ere the summer was gone they knew each other in this quiet nook as they might not have done after years of a stiffer and more formal acquaintance.

And especially to the Admiral and the Doctor were this closer intimacy and companionship of value. Each had a void in his life, as every man must have who with unexhausted strength steps out of the great race, but each by his society might help to fill up that of his neighbour. It is true that they had not much in common, but that is sometimes an aid rather than a bar to friendship. Each had been an enthusiast in his profession, and had retained all his interest in it. The Doctor still read from cover to cover his *Lancet* and his *Medical Journal,* attended all professional gatherings, worked himself into an alternate state of exaltation and depression over the results of the election of officers, and reserved for himself a den of his own, in which before rows of little round bottles full of glycerine, Canadian balsam, and staining agents, he still cut sections with a microtome, and peeped through his long, brass, old-fashioned microscope at the arcana of nature. With his typical face, clean shaven on lip and chin, with a firm mouth, a strong jaw, a steady eye, and two little white fluffs of whiskers, he could never be taken for anything but what he was, a high-class British medical consultant of the age of fifty or perhaps just a year or two older.

The Doctor, in his hey-day, had been cool over great things, but now, in his retirement, he was fussy over trifles. The man who had operated without the quiver of a finger, when not only his patient's life but his own reputation and future were at stake, was now shaken to the soul by a mislaid book or a careless maid. He remarked it himself, and knew the reason. "When Mary was alive," he would say, "she stood between me and the little troubles. I could brace myself for the big ones. My girls are as good as girls can be, but who can know a man as his wife knows him?" Then his memory would conjure up a tuft of brown hair and a single white, thin hand over a coverlet, and he would feel, as we have all felt, that if we do not live and know each other after death, then indeed we are tricked and betrayed by all the highest hopes and subtlest intuitions of our nature.

The Doctor had his compensations to make up for his loss. The great scales of Fate had been held on a level for him; for where in all great London could one find two sweeter girls, more loving, more intelligent, and more sympathetic than Clara and Ida Walker? So bright were they, so quick, so interested in all which interested him, that if it were possible for a man to be compensated for the loss of a good wife then Balthazar Walker might claim to be so.

Clara was tall and thin and supple, with a graceful, womanly figure. There was something stately and distinguished in her carriage, "queenly" her friends called her, while her critics described her as reserved and distant.

Such as it was, however, it was part and parcel of herself, for she was, and had always from her childhood been, different from any one around her. There was nothing gregarious in her nature. She thought with her own mind, saw with her own eyes, acted from her own impulse. Her face was pale, striking rather than pretty, but with two great dark eyes, so earnestly questioning, so quick in their transitions from joy to pathos, so swift in their comment upon every word and deed around her, that those eyes alone were to many more attractive than all the beauty of her younger sister. Hers was a strong, quiet soul, and it was her firm hand which had taken over the duties of her mother, had ordered the house, restrained the servants, comforted her father, and upheld her weaker sister, from the day of that great misfortune.

Ida Walker was a hand's breadth smaller than Clara, but was a little fuller in the face and plumper in the figure. She had light yellow hair, mischievous blue eyes with the light of humour ever twinkling in their depths, and a large, perfectly formed mouth, with that slight upward curve of the corners which goes with a keen appreciation of fun, suggesting even in repose that a latent smile is ever lurking at the edges of the lips. She was modern to the soles of her dainty little high-heeled shoes, frankly fond of dress and of pleasure, devoted to tennis and to comic opera, delighted with a dance, which came her way only too seldom, longing ever for some new excitement, and yet behind all this lighter side of her character a thoroughly good, healthy-minded English girl, the life and soul of the house, and the idol of her sister and her father. Such was the family at number two. A peep into the remaining villa and our introductions are complete.

Admiral Hay Denver did not belong to the florid, white-haired, hearty school of sea-dogs which is more common in works of fiction than in the Navy List. On the contrary, he was the representative of a much more common type which is the antithesis of the conventional sailor. He was a thin, hard-featured man, with an ascetic, acquiline cast of face, grizzled and hollow-cheeked, clean-shaven with the exception of the tiniest curved promontory of ash-coloured whisker. An observer, accustomed to classify men, might have put him down as a canon of the church with a taste for lay costume and a country life, or as the master of a large public school, who joined his scholars in their outdoor sports. His lips were firm, his chin prominent, he had a hard, dry eye, and his manner was precise and formal. Forty years of stern discipline had made him reserved and silent. Yet, when at his ease with an equal, he could readily assume a less quarter-deck style, and he had a fund of little, dry stories of the world and its ways which were of interest from one who had seen so many phases of life. Dry and spare, as lean as a jockey and as tough as whipcord, he might be seen any day swinging his silver-headed Malacca cane, and pacing along the suburban roads with the same measured gait with which he had been wont to tread the poop of his flagship. He wore a good service stripe upon his cheek, for on one side it was pitted and scarred where a spurt of gravel knocked up by a round-shot had struck him thirty years before, when he served in the Lancaster gun-battery. Yet he was hale and sound, and though he was fifteen years senior to his friend the Doctor, he might have passed as the younger man.

Mrs. Hay Denver's life had been a very broken one, and her record upon land represented a greater amount of endurance and self-sacrifice than his upon the sea. They had been together for four months after their marriage, and then had come a hiatus of four years, during which he was flitting about between St. Helena and the Oil Rivers in a gunboat. Then came a blessed year of peace and domesticity, to be followed by nine years, with only a three months' break, five upon the Pacific station, and four on the East Indian. After that was a respite in the shape of five years in the Channel Squadron, with periodical runs home, and then again he was off to the Mediterranean for three years and to Halifax for four. Now, at last, however, this old married couple, who were still almost strangers to one another, had come together in Norwood, where, if their short day had been chequered and broken, the evening at least promised to be sweet and mellow. In person Mrs. Hay Denver was tall and stout, with a bright, round, ruddy-cheeked face still pretty, with a gracious, matronly comeliness. Her whole life was a round of devotion and of love, which was divided between her husband and her only son, Harold.

This son it was who kept them in the neighbourhood of London, for the Admiral was as fond of ships and of salt water as ever, and was as happy in the sheets of a two-ton yacht as on the bridge of his sixteen-knot monitor. Had he been untied, the Devonshire or Hampshire coast would certainly have been his choice. There was Harold, however, and Harold's interests were their chief care. Harold was four-and-twenty now. Three years before he had been taken in hand by an acquaintance of his father's, the head of a considerable firm of stockbrokers, and fairly launched upon 'Change. His three hundred guinea entrance fee paid, his three sureties of five hundred pounds each found, his name approved by the Committee, and all other formalities complied with, he found himself whirling round, an insignificant unit, in the vortex of the money market of the world. There, under the guidance of his father's friend, he was instructed in the mysteries of bulling and of bearing, in the strange usages of 'Change in the intricacies of carrying over and of transferring. He learned to know where to place his clients' money, which of the jobbers would make a price in New Zealands, and which would touch nothing but American rails, which might be trusted and which shunned. All this, and much more, he mastered, and to such purpose that he soon began to prosper, to retain the clients who had been recommended to him, and to attract fresh ones. But the work was never congenial. He had inherited from his father his love of the air of heaven, his affection for a manly and natural existence. To act as middleman between the pursuer of wealth, and the wealth which he pursued, or to stand as a human barometer, registering the rise and fall of the great mammon pressure in the markets, was not the work for which Providence had placed those broad shoulders and strong limbs upon his well knit frame. His dark open face, too, with his straight Grecian nose, well opened brown eyes, and round black-curled head, were all those of a man who was fashioned for active physical work. Meanwhile he was popular with his fellow brokers, respected by his clients, and beloved at home, but his spirit was restless within him and his mind chafed unceasingly against his surroundings.

"Do you know, Willy," said Mrs. Hay Denver one evening as she stood behind her husband's chair, with her hand upon his shoulder, "I think sometimes that Harold is not quite happy."

"He looks happy, the young rascal," answered the Admiral, pointing with his cigar. It was after dinner, and through the open French window of the dining-room a clear view was to be had of the tennis court and the players. A set had just been finished, and young Charles Westmacott was hitting up the balls as high as he could send them in the middle of the ground. Doctor Walker and Mrs. Westmacott were pacing up and down the lawn, the lady waving her racket as she emphasized her remarks, and the Doctor listening with slanting head and little nods of agreement. Against the rails at the near end Harold was leaning in his flannels talking to the two sisters, who stood listening to him with their long dark shadows streaming down the lawn behind them. The girls were dressed alike in dark skirts, with light pink tennis blouses and pink bands on their straw hats, so that as they stood with the soft red of the setting sun tinging their faces, Clara, demure and quiet, Ida, mischievous and daring, it was a group which might have pleased the eye of a more exacting critic than the old sailor.

"Yes, he looks happy, mother," he repeated, with a chuckle. "It is not so long ago since it was you and I who were standing like that, and I don't remember that we were very unhappy either. It was croquet in our time, and the ladies had not reefed in their skirts quite so taut. What year would it be? Just before the commission of the *Penelope.*"

Mrs. Hay Denver ran her fingers through his grizzled hair. "It was when you came back in the *Antelope,* just before you got your step."

"Ah, the old *Antelope!* What a clipper she was! She could sail two points nearer the wind than anything of her tonnage in the service. You remember her, mother. You saw her come into Plymouth Bay. Wasn't she a beauty?"

"She was indeed, dear. But when I say that I think that Harold is not happy I mean in his daily life. Has it never struck you how thoughtful he is at times, and how absent-minded?"

"In love perhaps, the young dog. He seems to have found snug moorings now at any rate."

"I think that it is very likely that you are right, Willy," answered the mother seriously.

"But with which of them?"

"I cannot tell."

"Well, they are very charming girls, both of them.

But as long as he hangs in the wind between the two it cannot be serious. After all, the boy is four-and-twenty, and he made five hundred pounds last year. He is better able to marry than I was when I was lieutenant."

"I think that we can see which it is now," remarked the observant mother. Charles Westmacott had ceased to knock the tennis balls about, and was chatting with Clara Walker, while Ida and Harold Denver were still talking by the railing with little outbursts of laughter. Presently a fresh set was formed, and Doctor Walker, the odd man out, came through the wicket gate and strolled up the garden walk.

"Good evening, Mrs. Hay Denver," said he, raising his broad straw hat. "May I come in?"

"Good evening, Doctor! Pray do!"

"Try one of these," said the Admiral, holding out his cigar-case. "They are not bad. I got them on the Mosquito Coast. I was thinking of signalling to you, but you seemed so very happy out there."

"Mrs. Westmacott is a very clever woman," said the Doctor, lighting the cigar. "By the way, you spoke about the Mosquito Coast just now. Did you see much of the *Hyla* when you were out there?"

"No such name on the list," answered the seaman, with decision. "There's a *Hydra,* a harbour defense turret-ship, but she never leaves the home waters."

The Doctor laughed. "We live in two separate worlds," said he. "The *Hyla* is the little green tree frog, and Beale has founded some of his views on protoplasm upon the appearances of its nerve cells. It is a subject in which I take an interest."

"There were vermin of all sorts in the woods. When I have been on river service I have heard it at night like the engine-room when you are on the measured mile.

You can't sleep for the piping, and croaking, and chirping. Great Scott! what a woman that is! She was across the lawn in three jumps. She would have made a captain of the foretop in the old days."

"She is a very remarkable woman."

"A very cranky one."

"A very sensible one in some things," remarked Mrs. Hay Denver.

"Look at that now!" cried the Admiral, with a lunge of his forefinger at the Doctor. "You mark my words, Walker, if we don't look out that woman will raise a mutiny with her preaching. Here's my wife disaffected already, and your girls will be no better. We must combine, man, or there's an end of all discipline."

"No doubt she is a little excessive in her views," said the Doctor, "but in the main I think as she does."

"Bravo, Doctor!" cried the lady.

"What, turned traitor to your sex! We'll court-martial you as a deserter."

"She is quite right. The professions are not sufficiently open to women. They are still far too much circumscribed in their employments. They are feeble folk, the women who have to work for their bread—poor, unorganized, timid, taking as a favour what they might demand as a right. That is why their case is not more constantly before the public, for if their cry for redress was as great as their grievance it would fill the world to the exclusion of all others. It is all very well for us to be courteous to the rich, the refined, those to whom life is already made easy. It is a mere form, a trick of manner. If we are truly courteous, we shall stoop to lift up struggling womanhood when she really needs our help—when it is life and death to her whether she has it or not. And then to cant about it being unwomanly to work in the higher professions. It is womanly enough to starve, but unwomanly to use the brains which God has given them. Is it not a monstrous contention?"

The Admiral chuckled. "You are like one of these phonographs, Walker," said he; "you have had all this talked into you, and now you are reeling it off again. It's rank mutiny, every word of it, for man has his duties and woman has hers, but they are as separate as their natures are. I suppose that we shall have a woman hoisting her pennant on the flagship presently, and taking command of the Channel Squadron."

"Well, you have a woman on the throne taking command of the whole nation," remarked his wife; "and everybody is agreed that she does it better than any of the men."

The Admiral was somewhat staggered by this home-thrust. "That's quite another thing," said he.

"You should come to their next meeting. I am to take the chair. I have just promised Mrs. Westmacott that I will do so. But it has turned chilly, and it is time that the girls were indoors. Good night! I shall look out for you after breakfast for our constitutional, Admiral."

The old sailor looked after his friend with a twinkle in his eyes.

"How old is he, mother?"

"About fifty, I think."

"And Mrs. Westmacott?"

"I heard that she was forty-three."

The Admiral rubbed his hands, and shook with amusement. "We'll find one of these days that three and two make one," said he. "I'll bet you a new bonnet on it, mother."

The shadows had fallen now and the game been abandoned.

4
A Sister's Secret

"TELL ME, Miss Walker! You know how things should be. What would you say was a good profession for a young man of twenty-six who had had no education worth speaking about, and who is not very quick by nature?" The speaker was Charles Westmacott, and the time this same summer evening in the tennis ground, though the shadows had fallen now and the game been abandoned.

The girl glanced up at him, amused and surprised.

"Do you mean yourself?"

"Precisely."

"But how could I tell?"

"I have no one to advise me. I believe that you could do it better than any one. I feel confidence in your opinion."

"It is very flattering." She glanced up again at his earnest, questioning face, with its Saxon eyes and drooping flaxen moustache, in some doubt as to whether he might be joking. On the contrary, all his attention seemed to be concentrated upon her answer.

"It depends so much upon what you can do, you know. I do not know you sufficiently to be able to say what natural gifts you have." They were walking slowly across the lawn in the direction of the house.

"I have none. That is to say none worth mentioning. I have no memory and I am very slow."

"But you are very strong."

"Oh, if that goes for anything. I can put up a hundred-pound bar till further orders; but what sort of a calling is that?"

Some little joke about being called to the bar flickered up in Miss Walker's mind, but her companion was in such obvious earnest that she stifled down her inclination to laugh.

"I can do a mile on the cinder-track in 4:50 and across-country in 5:20, but how is that to help me? I might be a cricket professional, but it is not a very dignified position. Not that I care a straw about dignity, you know, but I should not like to hurt the old lady's feelings."

"Your aunt's?"

"Yes, my aunt's. My parents were killed in the Mutiny, you know, when I was a baby, and she has looked after me ever since. She has been very good to me. I'm sorry to leave her."

"But why should you leave her?" They had reached the garden gate, and the girl leaned her racket upon the top of it, looking up with grave interest at her big white-flannelled companion.

"It's Browning," said he.

"What!"

"Don't tell my aunt that I said it"—he sank his voice to a whisper—"I hate Browning."

Clara Walker rippled off into such a merry peal of laughter that he forgot the evil things which he had suffered from the poet, and burst out laughing too.

"I can't make him out," said he. "I try, but he is one too many. No doubt it is very stupid of me; I don't deny it. But as long as I cannot there is no use pretending that I can. And then of course she feels hurt, for she is very fond of him, and likes to read him aloud in the evenings. She is reading a piece now, *Pippa Passes,* and I assure you, Miss Walker, that I don't even know what the title means. You must think me a dreadful fool."

"But surely he is not so incomprehensible as all that?" she said, as an attempt at encouragement.

"He is very bad. There are some things, you know, which are fine. That ride of the three Dutchmen, and Hervé Riel and others, they are all right. But there was a piece we read last week. The first line stumped my aunt, and it takes a good deal to do that, for she rides very straight. 'Setebos and Setebos and Setebos.' That was the line."

"It sounds like a charm."

"No, it is a gentleman's name. Three gentlemen, I thought, at first, but my aunt says one. Then he goes on, 'Thinketh he dwelleth in the light of the moon.' It was a very trying piece."

Clara Walker laughed again.

"You must not think of leaving your aunt," she said. "Think how lonely she would be without you."

"Well, yes, I have thought of that. But you must remember that my aunt is to all intents hardly middle-aged, and a very eligible person. I don't think that her dislike to mankind extends to individuals. She might form new ties, and then I should be a third wheel in the coach. It was all very well as long as I was only a boy, when her first husband was alive."

"But, good gracious, you don't mean that Mrs. Westmacott is going to marry again?" gasped Clara.

The young man glanced down at her with a question in his eyes. "Oh, it is only a remote possibility, you know," said he. "Still, of course, it might happen, and I should like to know what I ought to turn my hand to."

"I wish I could help you," said Clara. "But I really know very little about such things. However, I could talk to my father, who knows a very great deal of the world."

"I wish you would. I should be so glad if you would."

"Then I certainly will. And now I must say good-night, Mr. Westmacott, for papa will be wondering where I am."

"Good-night, Miss Walker." He pulled off his flannel cap, and stalked away through the gathering darkness.

Clara had imagined that they had been the last on the lawn, but, looking back from the steps which led up to the French windows, she saw two dark figures moving across towards the house. As they came nearer she could distinguish that they were Harold Denver and her sister Ida. The murmur of their voices rose up to her ears, and then the musical little child-like laugh which she knew so well. "I am so delighted," she heard her sister say. "So pleased and proud. I had no idea of it. Your words were such a surprise and a joy to me. Oh, I am so glad."

"Is that you, Ida?"

"Oh, there is Clara. I must go in, Mr. Denver. Good-night!"

There were a few whispered words, a laugh from Ida, and a "Good-night, Miss Walker," out of the darkness. Clara took her sister's hand, and they passed together through the long folding window. The Doctor had gone into his study, and the dining-room was empty. A single small red lamp upon the sideboard was reflected tenfold by the plate about it and the mahogany beneath it, though its single wick cast but a feeble light into the large, dimly shadowed room. Ida danced off to the big central lamp, but Clara put her hand upon her arm. "I rather like this quiet light," said she. "Why should we not have a chat?" She sat in the Doctor's large red plush chair, and her sister cuddled down upon the footstool at her feet, glancing up at her elder sister with a smile upon her lips and a mischievous gleam in her eyes. There was a shade of anxiety in Clara's face, which cleared away as she gazed into her sister's frank blue eyes.

"Have you anything to tell me, dear?" she asked.

Ida gave a little pout and shrug to her shoulder. "The Solicitor-General then opened the case for the prosecution," said she. "You are going to cross-examine me, Clara, so don't deny it. I do wish you would have that grey satin foulard of yours done up. With a little trimming and a new white vest it would look as good as new, and it is really very dowdy."

"You were quite late upon the lawn," said the inexorable Clara.

"Yes, I was rather. So were you. Have you anything to tell me?" She broke away into her merry musical laugh.

"I was chatting with Mr. Westmacott."

"And I was chatting with Mr. Denver. By the way, Clara, now tell me truly, what do you think of Mr. Denver? Do you like him? Honestly now!"

"I like him very much indeed. I think that he is one of the most gentlemanly, modest, manly young men that I have ever known. So now, dear, have you nothing to tell me?" Clara smoothed down her sister's golden hair with a motherly gesture, and stooped her face to catch the expected confidence. She could wish nothing better than that Ida should be the wife of Harold Denver, and from the words which she had overheard as they left the lawn that evening, she could not doubt that there was some understanding between them.

But there came no confession from Ida. Only the same mischievous smile and amused gleam in her deep blue eyes.

"That grey foulard dress——" she began.

"Oh, you little tease! Come now, I will ask you what you have just asked me. Do you like Harold Denver?"

"Oh, he's a darling!"

"Ida!"

"Well, you asked me. That's what I think of him. And now, you dear old inquisitive, you will get nothing more out of me; so you must wait and not be too curious. I'm going off to see what papa is doing." She sprang to her feet, threw her arms round her sister's neck, gave her a final squeeze, and was gone. A chorus from *Olivette,* sung in her clear contralto, grew fainter and fainter until it ended in the slam of a distant door.

But Clara Walker still sat in the dim-lit room with her chin upon her hands, and her dreamy eyes looking out into the gathering gloom. It was the duty of her, a maiden, to play the part of a mother—to guide another in paths which her own steps had not yet trodden. Since her mother died not a thought had been given to herself, all was for her father and sister. In her own eyes she was herself very plain, and she knew that her manner was often ungracious when she would most wish to be gracious. She saw her face as the glass reflected it, but she did not see the changing play of expression which gave it its charm—the infinite pity, the sympathy, the sweet womanliness which drew towards her all who were in doubt and in trouble, even as poor slow-moving Charles Westmacott had been drawn to her that night. She was herself, she thought, outside the pale of love. But it was very different with Ida, merry, little, quick-witted, bright-faced Ida. She was born for love. It was her inheritance. But she was young and innocent. She must not be allowed to venture too far without help in those dangerous waters. Some understanding there was between her and Harold Denver. In her heart of hearts Clara, like every good woman, was a match-maker, and already she had chosen Denver of all men as the one to whom she could most safely confide Ida. He had talked to her more than once on the serious topics of life, on his aspirations, on what a man could do to leave the world better for his presence. She knew that he was a man of a noble nature, high-minded and earnest. And yet she did not like this secrecy, this disinclination upon the part of one so frank and honest as Ida to tell her what was passing. She would wait, and if she got the opportunity next day she would lead Harold Denver himself on to this topic. It was possible that she might learn from him what her sister had refused to tell her.

"Why, by George, it is that woman!"

5
A Naval Conquest

It was the habit of the Doctor and the Admiral to accompany each other upon a morning ramble between breakfast and lunch. The dwellers in those quiet tree-lined roads were accustomed to see the two figures, the long, thin, austere seaman, and the short, bustling, tweed-clad physician, pass and repass with such regularity that a stopped clock has been reset by them. The Admiral took two steps to his companion's three, but the younger man was the quicker, and both were equal to a good four and a half miles an hour.

It was a lovely summer day which followed the events which have been described. The sky was of the deepest blue, with a few white, fleecy clouds drifting lazily across it, and the air was filled with the low drone of insects or with a sudden sharper note as bee or bluefly shot past with its quivering, long-drawn hum, like an insect tuning-fork. As the friends topped each rise which leads up to the Crystal Palace, they could see the dun clouds of London stretching along the northern sky-line, with spire or dome breaking through the low-lying haze. The Admiral was in high spirits, for the morning post had brought good news to his son.

"It is wonderful, Walker," he was saying, "positively wonderful, the way that boy of mine has gone ahead during the last three years. We heard from Pearson to-day. Pearson is the senior partner, you know, and my boy the junior—Pearson and Denver the firm. Cunning old dog is Pearson, as cute and as greedy as a Rio shark. Yet he goes off for a fortnight's leave, and puts my boy in full charge, with all that immense business in his hands, and a free hand to do what he likes with it. How's that for confidence, and he only three years upon 'Change?"

"Any one would confide in him. His face is a surety," said the Doctor.

"Go on, Walker!" The Admiral dug his elbow at him. "You know my weak side. Still it's truth all the same. I've been blessed with a good wife and a good son, and maybe I relish them the more for having been cut off from them so long. I have much to be thankful for!"

"And so have I. The best two girls that ever stepped. There's Clara, who has learned up as much medicine as would give her the L.S.A., simply in order that she may sympathize with me in my work. But hullo, what is this coming along?"

"All drawing and the wind astern!" cried the Admiral. "Fourteen knots if it's one. Why, by George, it is that woman!"

A rolling cloud of yellow dust had streamed round the curve of the road, and from the heart of it had emerged a high tandem tricycle flying along at a breakneck pace. In front sat Mrs. Westmacott clad in a heather tweed pea-jacket, a skirt which just passed her knees and a pair of thick gaiters of the same material. She had a great bundle of red papers under her arm, while Charles, who sat behind her clad in Norfolk jacket and knickerbockers, bore a similar roll protruding from either pocket. Even as they watched, the pair eased up, the lady sprang off, impaled one of her bills upon the garden railing of an empty house, and then jumping on to her seat again was about to hurry onwards when her nephew drew her attention to the two gentlemen upon the footpath.

"Oh, now, really I didn't notice you," said she, taking a few turns of the treadle and steering the machine across to them. "Is it not a beautiful morning?"

"Lovely," answered the Doctor. "You seem to be very busy."

"I *am* very busy." She pointed to the coloured paper which still fluttered from the railing. "We have been pushing our propaganda, you see. Charles and I have been at it since seven o'clock. It is about our meeting. I wish it to be a great success. See!" She smoothed out one of the bills, and the Doctor read his own name in great black letters across the bottom.

"We don't forget our chairman, you see. Everybody is coming. Those two dear little old maids opposite, the Williamses, held out for some time; but I have their promise now. Admiral, I am sure that you wish us well."

"Hum! I wish you no harm, ma'am."

"You will come on the platform?"

"I'll be— No, I don't think I can do that."

"To our meeting, then?"

"No, ma'am; I don't go out after dinner."

"Oh, yes, you will come. I will call in if I may, and chat it over with you when you come home. We have not breakfasted yet. Good-bye!" There was a whir of wheels, and the yellow cloud rolled away down the road again. By some legerdemain the Admiral found that he was clutching in his right hand one of the obnoxious bills. He crumpled it up, and threw it into the roadway.

"I'll be hanged if I go, Walker," said he, as he resumed his walk. "I've never been hustled into doing a thing yet, whether by woman or man."

"I am not a betting man," answered the Doctor, "but I rather think that the odds are in favour of your going."

The Admiral had hardly got home, and had just seated himself in his dining-room, when the attack upon him was renewed. He was slowly and lovingly unfolding *The Times* preparatory to the long read which led up to luncheon, and had even got so far as to fasten his golden pince-nez on to his thin, high-bridged nose, when he heard a crunching of gravel, and, looking over the top of his paper, saw Mrs. Westmacott coming up the garden walk. She was still dressed in the singular custume which offended the sailor's old-fashioned notions of propriety, but he could not deny, as he looked at her, that she was a very fine woman. In many climes he had looked upon women of all shades and ages, but never upon a more clear-cut, handsome face, nor a more erect, supple, and womanly figure. He ceased to glower as he gazed at her, and the frown smoothed away from his rugged brow.

"May I come in?" said she, framing herself in the open window, with a background of green sward and blue sky. "I feel like an invader deep in an enemy's country."

"It is a very welcome invasion, ma'am," said he, clearing his throat and pulling at his high collar. "Try this garden chair. What is there that I can do for you? Shall I ring and let Mrs. Denver know that you are here?"

"Pray do not trouble, Admiral. I only looked in with reference to our little chat this morning. I wish that you would give us your powerful support at our coming meeting for the improvement of the condition of woman."

"No, ma'am, I can't do that." He pursed up his lips and shook his grizzled head.

"And why not?"

"Against my principles, ma'am."

"But why?"

"Because woman has her duties and man has his. I may be old-fashioned, but that is my view. Why, what is the world coming to? I was saying to Dr. Walker only last night that we shall have a woman wanting to command the Channel Fleet next."

"That is one of the few professions which cannot be improved," said Mrs. Westmacott, with her sweetest smile. "Poor woman must still look to man for protection."

"I don't like these new-fangled ideas, ma'am. I tell you honestly that I don't. I like discipline, and I think every one is the better for it. Women have got a great deal which they had not in the days of our fathers. They have universities all for themselves, I am told, and there are women doctors, I hear. Surely they should rest contented. What more can they want?"

"You are a sailor, and sailors are always chivalrous. If you could see how things really are, you would change your position. What are the poor things to do? There are so many of them and so few things to which they can turn their hands. Governesses? But there are hardly any situations. Music and drawing? There is not one in fifty who has any special talent in that direction. Medicine? It is still surrounded with difficulties for women, and it takes many years and a small fortune to qualify. Nursing? It is hard work ill paid, and none but the strongest can stand it. What would you have them do then, Admiral? Sit down and starve?"

"Tut, tut! It is not so bad as that."

"The pressure is terrible. Advertise for a lady companion at ten shillings a week, which is less than a cook's wage, and see how many answers you get. There is no hope, no outlook, for these struggling thousands. Life is a dull, sordid struggle, leading down to a cheerless old age. Yet when we try to bring some little ray of hope, some chance, however distant, of something better, we are told by chivalrous gentlemen that it is against their principles to help."

The Admiral winced, but shook his head in dissent.

"There is banking, the law, veterinary surgery, government offices, the civil service, all these at least should be thrown freely open to women, if they have brains enough to compete successfully for them. Then if woman were unsuccessful it would be her own fault, and the majority of the population of this country could no longer complain that they live under a different law to the minority, and that they are held down in poverty and serfdom, with every road to independence sealed to them."

"What would you propose to do, ma'am?"

"To set the more obvious injustices right, and so to pave the way for a reform. Now look at that man digging in the field. I know him. He can neither read nor write, he is steeped in whisky, and he has as much intelligence as the potatoes that he is digging. Yet the man has a vote, can possibly turn the scale of an election, and may help to decide the policy of this empire. Now, to take the nearest example, here am I, a woman who have had some education, who have travelled, and who have seen and studied the institutions of many countries. I hold considerable property, and I pay more in imperial taxes than that man spends in whisky, which is saying a great deal, and yet I have no more direct influence upon the disposal of the money which I pay than that fly which creeps along the wall. Is that right? Is it fair?"

The Admiral moved uneasily in his chair. "Yours is an exceptional case," said he.

"But no woman has a voice. Consider that the women are a majority of the nation. Yet if there was a question of legislation upon which all women were agreed upon one side and all the men upon the other, it would appear that the matter was settled unanimously when more than half the population were opposed to it. Is that right?"

Again the Admiral wriggled. It was very awkward for the gallant seaman to have a handsome woman opposite to him, bombarding him with questions to none of which he could find an answer. "Couldn't even get the tompions out of his guns," as he explained the matter to the Doctor that evening.

"Now those are really the points that we shall lay stress upon at the meeting. The free and complete opening of the professions, the final abolition of the zenana I call it, and the franchise to all women who pay Queen's taxes above a certain sum. Surely there is nothing unreasonable in that. Nothing which could offend your principles. We shall have medicine, law, and the church all rallying that night for the protection of woman. Is the navy to be the one profession absent?"

The Admiral jumped out of his chair with an evil word in his throat. "There, there, ma'am," he cried.

"Drop it for a time. I have heard enough. You've turned me a point or two. I won't deny it. But let it stand at that. I will think it over."

"Certainly, Admiral. We would not hurry you in your decision. But we still hope to see you on our platform." She rose and moved about in her lounging masculine fashion from one picture to another, for the walls were thickly covered with reminiscences of the Admiral's voyages.

"Hullo!" said she. "Surely this ship would have furled all her lower canvas and reefed her topsails if she found herself on a lee shore with the wind on her quarter."

"Of course she would. The artist was never past Gravesend, I swear. It's the *Penelope* as she was on the 14th of June, 1857, in the throat of the Straits of Banca, with the Island of Banca on the starboard bow, and Sumatra on the port. He painted it from description, but of course, as you very sensibly say, all was snug below and she carried storm sails and double-reefed topsails, for it was blowing a cyclone from the sou'east. I compliment you, ma'am, I do indeed!"

"Oh, I have done a little sailoring myself—as much as a woman can aspire to, you know. This is the Bay of Funchal. What a lovely frigate!"

"Lovely, you say! Ah, she was lovely! That is the *Andromeda.* I was a mate aboard of her—sub-lieutenant they call it now, though I like the old name best."

"What a lovely rake her masts have, and what a curve to her bows! She must have been a clipper."

The old sailor rubbed his hands and his eyes glistened. His old ships bordered close upon his wife and his son in his affections.

"I know Funchal," said the lady carelessly. "A couple of years ago I had a seven-ton cutter-rigged yacht, the *Banshee,* and we ran over to Madeira from Falmouth."

"You, ma'am, in a seven-tonner?"

"With a couple of Cornish lads for a crew. Oh, it was glorious! A fortnight right out in the open, with no worries, no letters, no callers, no petty thoughts, nothing but the grand works of God, the tossing sea and the great silent sky. They talk of riding, indeed, I am fond of horses, too, but what is there to compare with the swoop of a little craft as she pitches down the long steep side of a wave, and then the quiver and spring as she is tossed upwards again? Oh, if our souls could transmigrate I'd be a seamew above all birds that fly! But I keep you, Admiral. Adieu!"

The old sailor was too transported with sympathy to say a word. He could only shake her broad muscular hand. She was half-way down the garden path before she heard him calling her, and saw his grizzled head and weather-stained face looking out from behind the curtains.

"You may put me down for the platform," he cried, and vanished abashed behind the curtain of his *Times,* where his wife found him at lunch time.

"I hear that you have had quite a long chat with Mrs. Westmacott," said she.

"Yes, and I think that she is one of the most sensible women that I ever knew."

"Except on the woman's rights question, of course."

"Oh, I don't know. She had a good deal to say for herself on that also. In fact, mother, I have taken a platform ticket for her meeting."

"Don't, for goodness' sake, begin to be languid and young ladyish!"

6
An Old Story

But this was not to be the only eventful conversation which Mrs. Westmacott held that day, nor was the Admiral the only person in The Wilderness who was destined to find his opinions considerably changed. Two neighbouring families, the Winslows from Anerley, and the Cumberbatches from Gipsy Hill, had been invited to tennis by Mrs. Westmacott, and the lawn was gay in the evening with the blazers of the young men and the bright dresses of the girls. To the older people, sitting round in their wicker-work garden chairs, the darting, stooping, springing white figures, the sweep of skirts, and twinkle of canvas shoes, the click of the rackets and sharp whiz of the balls, with the continual "fifteen love—fifteen all!" of the marker, made up a merry and exhilarating scene. To see their sons and daughters so flushed and healthy and happy, gave them also a reflected glow, and it was hard to say who had most pleasure from the game, those who played or those who watched.

Mrs. Westmacott had just finished a set when she caught a glimpse of Clara Walker sitting alone at the farther end of the ground. She ran down the court, cleared the net to the amazement of the visitors, and seated herself beside her. Clara's reserved and refined nature shrank somewhat from the boisterous frankness and strange manners of the widow, and yet her feminine instinct told her that beneath all her peculiarities there lay much that was good and noble. She smiled up at her, therefore, and nodded a greeting.

"Why aren't you playing, then? Don't, for goodness' sake, begin to be languid and young ladyish! When you give up active sports you give up youth."

"I have played a set, Mrs. Westmacott."

"That's right, my dear." She sat down beside her, and tapped her upon the arm with her tennis racket. "I like you, my dear, and I am going to call you Clara. You are not as aggressive as I should wish, Clara, but still I like you very much. Self-sacrifice is all very well, you know, but we have had rather too much of it on our side, and should like to see a little on the other. What do you think of my nephew Charles?"

The question was so sudden and unexpected that Clara gave quite a jump in her chair. "I—I—I hardly ever have thought of your nephew Charles."

"No? Oh, you must think him well over, for I want to speak to you about him."

"To me? But why?"

"It seemed to me most delicate. You see, Clara, the matter stands in this way. It is quite possible that I may soon find myself in a completely new sphere of life, which will involve fresh duties and make it impossible for me to keep up a household which Charles can share."

Clara stared. Did this mean that she was about to marry again? What else could it point to?

"Therefore Charles must have a household of his own. That is obvious. Now, I don't approve of bachelor establishments. Do you?"

"Really, Mrs. Westmacott, I have never thought of the matter."

"Oh, you little sly puss! Was there ever a girl who never thought of the matter? I think that a young man of six-and-twenty ought to be married."

Clara felt very uncomfortable. The awful thought had come upon her that this ambassadress had come to her as a proxy with a proposal of marriage. But how could that be? She had not spoken more than three or four times with her nephew, and knew nothing more of him than he had told her on the evening before. It was impossible, then. And yet what could this aunt mean by this discussion of his private affairs?

"Do you not think yourself," she persisted, "that a young man of six-and-twenty is better married?"

"I should think that he is old enough to decide for himself."

"Yes, yes. He has done so. But Charles is just a little shy, just a little slow in expressing himself. I thought that I would pave the way for him. Two women can arrange these things so much better. Men sometimes have a difficulty in making themselves clear."

"I really hardly follow you, Mrs. Westmacott," cried Clara in despair.

"He has no profession. But he has nice tastes. He reads Browning every night. And he is most amazingly strong. When he was younger we used to put on the gloves together, but I cannot persuade him to now, for he says he cannot play light enough. I should allow him five hundred, which should be enough at first."

"My dear Mrs. Westmacott," cried Clara, "I assure you that I have not the least idea what it is that you are talking of."

"Do you think your sister Ida would have my nephew Charles?"

Her sister Ida? Quite a little thrill of relief and of pleasure ran through her at the thought. Ida and Charles Westmacott. She had never thought of it. And yet they had been a good deal together. They had played tennis. They had shared the tandem tricycle. Again came the thrill of joy, and close at its heels the cold questionings of conscience. Why this joy? What was the source of it? Was it that deep down, somewhere pushed back in the black recesses of the soul, there was the thought lurking that if Charles prospered in his wooing then Harold Denver would still be free? How mean, how unmaidenly, how unsisterly the thought! She crushed it down and thrust it aside, but still it would push up its wicked little head. She crimsoned with shame at her own baseness, as she turned once more to her companion.

"I really do not know," she said.

"She is not engaged?"

"Not that I know of."

"You speak hesitatingly."

"Because I am not sure. But he may ask. She cannot but be flattered."

"Quite so. I tell him that it is the most practical compliment which a man can pay to a woman. He is a little shy, but when he sets himself to do it he will do it. He is very much in love with her, I assure you. These little lively people always do attract the slow and heavy ones, which is nature's device for the neutralizing of bores. But they are all going in. I think if you will allow me that I will just take the opportunity to tell him that, as far as you know, there is no positive obstacle in the way."

"As far as I know," Clara repeated, as the widow moved away to where the players were grouped round the net, or sauntering slowly towards the house. She rose to follow her, but her head was in a whirl with new thoughts, and she sat down again. Which would be best for Ida, Harold or Charles? She thought it over with as much solicitude as a mother who plans for her only child. Harold had seemed to her to be in many ways the noblest and the best young man whom she had known. If ever she was to love a man it would be such a man as that. But she must not think of herself. She had reasons to believe that both these men loved her sister. Which would be the best for her? But perhaps the matter was already decided. She could not forget the scrap of conversation which she had heard the night before, nor the secret which her sister had refused to confide to her. If Ida would not tell her, there was but one person who could. She raised her eyes, and there was Harold Denver standing before her.

"You were lost in your thoughts," said he, smiling. "I hope that they were pleasant ones."

"Oh, I was planning," said she, rising. "It seems rather a waste of time as a rule, for things have a way of working themselves out just as you least expect."

"What were you planning, then?"

"The future."

"Whose?"

"Oh, my own and Ida's."

"And was I included in your joint futures?"

"I hope all our friends were included."

"Don't go in," said he, as she began to move slowly towards the house. "I wanted to have a word. Let us stroll up and down the lawn. Perhaps you are cold. If you are, I could bring you out a shawl."

"Oh, no, I am not cold."

"I was speaking to your sister Ida last night." She noticed that there was a slight quiver in his voice, and, glancing up at his dark, clear-cut face, she saw that he was very grave. She felt that it was settled, that he had come to ask her for her sister's hand.

"She is a charming girl," said he, after a pause.

"Indeed she is," cried Clara warmly. "And no one who has not lived with her and known her intimately can tell how charming and good she is. She is like a sunbeam in the house."

"No one who was not good could be so absolutely happy as she seems to be. Heaven's last gift, I think, is a maid so pure and a spirit so high that it is unable even to see what is impure and evil in the world around us. For as long as we can see it, how can we be truly happy?"

"She has a deeper side also. She does not turn it to the world, and it is not natural that she should, for she is very young. But she thinks, and has aspirations of her own."

"You cannot admire her more than I do. Indeed, Miss Walker, I only ask to be brought into nearer relationship with her, and to feel that there is a permanent bond between us."

It had come at last. For a moment her heart was numbed within her, and then a flood of sisterly love carried all before it. Down with that dark thought which would try to raise its unhallowed head! She turned to Harold with sparkling eyes and words of pleasure upon her lips.

"I should wish to be near and dear to both of you," said he, as he took her hand. "I should wish Ida to be my sister, and you my wife."

She said nothing. She only stood looking at him with parted lips and great, dark, questioning eyes. The lawn had vanished away, the sloping gardens, the brick villas, the darkening sky with half a pale moon beginning to show over the chimney-tops. All was gone, and she was only conscious of a dark, earnest, pleading face, and of a voice, far away, disconnected from herself, the voice of a man telling a woman how he loved her. He was unhappy, said the voice, his life was a void; there was but one thing that could save him; he had come to the parting of the ways, here lay happiness and honour, and all that was high and noble; there lay the soul-killing round, the lonely life, the base pursuit of money, the sordid, selfish aims. He needed but the hand of the woman that he loved to lead him into the better path. And how he loved her this life would show. He loved her for her sweetness, for her womanliness, for her strength. He had need of her. Would she not come to him? And then of a sudden as she listened it came home to her that the man was Harold Denver, and that she was the woman, and that all God's work was very beautiful—the green sward beneath her feet, the rustling leaves, the long orange slashes in the western sky. She spoke; she scarce knew what the broken words were, but she saw the light of joy shine out on his face, and her hand was still in his as they wandered amid the twilight. They said no more now, but only wandered and felt each other's presence. All was fresh around them, familiar and yet new, tinged with the beauty of their new-found happiness.

"Did you not know it before?" he asked.

"I did not dare to think it."

"What a mask of ice I must wear! How could a man

feel as I have done without showing it? Your sister at least knew."

"Ida!"

"It was last night. She began to praise you, I said what I felt, and then in an instant it was all out."

"But what could you—what *could* you see in me? Oh, I do pray that you may not repent it!" The gentle heart was ruffled amid its joy by the thought of its own unworthiness.

"Repent it! I feel that I am a saved man. You do not know how degrading this city life is, how debasing, and yet how absorbing. Money for ever clinks in your ear. You can think of nothing else. From the bottom of my heart I hate it, and yet how can I draw back without bringing grief to my dear old father? There was but one way in which I could defy the taint, and that was by having a home influence so pure and so high that it may brace me up against all that draws me down. I have felt that influence already. I know that when I am talking to you I am a better man. It is you who must go with me through life, or I must walk for ever alone."

"Oh, Harold, I am so happy!" Still they wandered amid the darkening shadows, while one by one the stars peeped out in the blue-black sky above them. At last a chill night wind blew up from the east, and brought them back to the realities of life.

"You must go in. You will be cold."

"My father will wonder where I am. Shall I say anything to him?"

"If you like, my darling. Or I will in the morning. I must tell my mother to-night. I know how delighted she will be."

"I do hope so."

"Let me take you up the garden path. It is so dark. Your lamp is not lit yet. There is the window. Till to-morrow, then, dearest."

"Till to-morrow, Harold."

"My own darling!" He stooped, and their lips met for the first time. Then, as she pushed open the folding windows she heard his quick, firm step as it passed down the gravelled path. A lamp was lit as she entered the room, and there was Ida, dancing about like a mischievous little fairy in front of her.

"And have you anything to tell me?" she asked, with a solemn face. Then, suddenly throwing her arms round her sister's neck, "Oh, you dear, dear old Clara! I am so pleased. I am so pleased."

Mile after mile they flew.

7

"Venit Tandem Felicitas"

IT was just days after the Doctor and the Admiral had congratulated each other upon the closer tie which was to unite their two families, and to turn their friendship into something even dearer and more intimate, that Miss Ida Walker received a letter which caused her some surprise and considerable amusement. It was dated from next door, and was handed in by the red-headed page after breakfast.

"Dear Miss Ida," began this curious document, and then relapsed suddenly into the third person. "Mr. Charles Westmacott hopes that he may have the extreme pleasure of a ride with Miss Ida Walker upon his tandem tricycle. Mr. Charles Westmacott will bring it round in half an hour. You in front. Yours very truly, Charles Westmacott." The whole was written in a large, loose-jointed, and school-boyish hand, very thin on the up strokes and thick on the down, as though care and pains had gone to the fashioning of it.

Strange as was the form, the meaning was clear enough; so Ida hastened to her room, and had hardly slipped on her light grey cycling dress when she saw the tandem with its large occupant at the door. He handed her up to her saddle with a more solemn and thoughtful face than was usual with him, and a few moments later they were flying along the beautiful, smooth suburban roads in the direction of Forest Hill. The great limbs of the athlete made the heavy machine spring and quiver with every stroke; while the mignon grey figure with the laughing face, and the golden curls blowing from under the little pink-banded straw hat, simply held firmly to her perch, and let the treadles whirl round beneath her feet. Mile after mile they flew, the wind beating in her face, the trees dancing past in two long ranks on either side, until they had passed round Croydon and were approaching Norwood once more from the further side.

"Aren't you tired?" she asked, glancing over her shoulder and turning towards him a little pink ear, a fluffy golden curl, and one blue eye twinkling from the very corner of its lid.

"Not a bit. I am just getting my swing."

"Isn't it wonderful to be strong? You always remind me of a steam engine."

"Why a steam engine?"

"Well, because it is so powerful, and reliable, and unreasoning. Well, I didn't mean that last, you know, but—but—you know what I mean. What is the matter with you?"

"Why?"

"Because you have something on your mind. You have not laughed once."

He broke into a gruesome laugh. "I am quite jolly," said he.

"Oh, no, you are not. And why did you write me such a dreadfully stiff letter?"

"There now," he cried, "I was sure it was stiff. I said it was absurdly stiff."

"Then why write it?"

"It wasn't my own composition."

"Whose then? Your aunt's?"

"Oh, no. It was a person of the name of Slattery."

"Goodness! Who is he?"

"I knew it would come out, I felt that it would. You've heard of Slattery the author?"

"Never."

"He is wonderful at expressing himself. He wrote a book called *The Secret Solved; or, Letter-writing Made Easy*. It gives you models of all sorts of letters."

Ida burst out laughing. "So you actually copied one."

"It was to invite a young lady to a picnic, but I set to work and soon got it changed so that it would do very well. Slattery seems never to have asked any one to ride a tandem. But when I had written it, it seemed so dreadfully stiff that I had to put a little beginning and end of my own, which seemed to brighten it up a good deal."

"I thought there was something funny about the beginning and end."

"Did you? Fancy your noticing the difference in style. How quick you are! I am very slow at things like that. I ought to have been a woodman, or game-keeper, or something. I was made on those lines. But I have found something now."

"What is that, then?"

"Ranching. I have a chum in Texas, and he says it is a rare life. I am to buy a share in his business. It is all in the open air—shooting, and riding, and sport. Would it—would it inconvenience you much, Ida, to come out there with me?"

Ida nearly fell off her perch in her amazement. The only words of which she could think were "My goodness me!" so she said them.

"If it would not upset your plans, or change your

arrangements in any way." He had slowed down and let go of the steering handle, so that the great machine crawled aimlessly about from one side of the road to the other. "I know very well that I am not clever or anything of that sort, but still I would do all I can to make you very happy. Don't you think that in time you might come to like me a little bit?"

Ida gave a cry of fright. "I won't like you if you run me against a brick wall," she said, as the machine rasped up against the curb. "Do attend to the steering."

"Yes, I will. But tell me, Ida, whether you will come with me."

"Oh, I don't know. It's too absurd! How can we talk about such things when I cannot see you? You speak to the nape of my neck, and then I have to twist my head round to answer."

"I know. That was why I put 'You in front' upon my letter. I thought that it would make it easier. But if you would prefer it I will stop the machine, and then you can sit round and talk about it."

"Good gracious!" cried Ida. "Fancy our sitting face to face on a motionless tricycle in the middle of the road, and all the people looking out of their windows at us!"

"It would look rather funny, wouldn't it? Well, then, suppose that we both get off and push the tandem along in front of us?"

"Oh, no, this is better than that."

"Or I could carry the thing."

Ida burst out laughing. "That would be more absurd still."

"Then we will go quietly, and I will look out for the steering. I won't talk about it at all if you would rather not. But I really do love you very much, and you would make me happy if you came to Texas with me, and I think that perhaps after a time I could make you happy too."

"But your aunt?"

"Oh, she would like it very much. I can understand that your father might not like to lose you. I'm sure I wouldn't either, if I were he. But after all, America is not very far off nowadays, and is not so very wild. We would take a grand piano, and—and—a copy of Browning. And Denver and his wife would come over to see us. We should be quite a family party. It would be jolly."

Ida sat listening to the stumbling words and awkward phrases which were whispered from the back of her, but there was something in Charles Westmacott's clumsiness of speech which was more moving than the words of the most eloquent of pleaders. He paused, he stammered, he caught his breath between the words, and he blurted out in little blunt phrases all the hopes of his heart. If love had not come to her yet, there was at least pity and sympathy, which are nearly akin to it. Wonder there was also that one so weak and frail as she should shake this strong man so, should have the whole course of his life waiting for her decision. Her left hand was on the cushion at her side. He leaned forward and took it gently in his own. She did not try to draw it back from him.

"May I have it," said he, "for life?"

"Oh, do attend to your steering," said she, smiling round at him; "and don't say any more about this to-day. Please don't!"

"When shall I know, then?"

"Oh, to-night, to-morrow, I don't know. I must ask Clara. Talk about something else."

And they did talk about something else; but her left hand was still enclosed in his, and he knew, without asking again, that all was well.

8
Shadows Before

MRS. WESTMACOTT's great meeting for the enfranchisement of woman had passed over, and it had been a triumphant success. All the maids and matrons of the southern suburbs had rallied at her summons, there was an influential platform with Dr. Balthazar Walker in the chair, and Admiral Hay Denver among his more prominent supporters. One benighted male had come in from the outside darkness and had jeered from the further end of the hall, but he had been called to order by the chair, petrified by indignant glances from the unenfranchised around him, and finally escorted to the door by Charles Westmacott. Fiery resolutions were passed, to be forwarded to a large number of leading statesmen, and the meeting broke up with the conviction that a shrewd blow had been struck for the cause of woman.

But there was one woman at least to whom the meeting and all that was connected with it had brought anything but pleasure. Clara Walker watched with a heavy heart the friendship and close intimacy which had sprung up between her father and the widow. From week to week it had increased until no day ever passed without their being together. The coming meeting had been the excuse for these continual interviews, but now the meeting was over, and still the Doctor would refer every point which rose to the judgment of his neighbour. He would talk, too, to his two daughters of her strength of character, her decisive mind, and of the necessity of their cultivating her acquaintance and following her example, until at last it had become his most common topic of conversation.

All this might have passed as merely the natural pleasure which an elderly man might take in the society of an intelligent and handsome woman, but there were other points which seemed to Clara to give it a deeper meaning. She could not forget that when Charles Westmacott had spoken to her one night he had alluded to the possibility of his aunt marrying again. He must have known or noticed something before he would speak upon such a subject. And then again Mrs. Westmacott had herself said that she hoped to change her style of living shortly and take over completely new duties. What could that mean except that she expected to marry? And whom? She seemed to see few friends outside their own little circle. She must have alluded to her father. It was a hateful thought, and yet it must be faced.

One evening the Doctor had been rather late at his neighbour's. He used to go into the Admiral's after dinner, but now he turned more frequently in the other direction. When he returned Clara was sitting alone in the drawing-room reading a magazine. She sprang up as he entered, pushed forward his chair, and ran to fetch his slippers.

"You are looking a little pale, dear," he remarked.

"Oh, no, papa, I am very well."

"All well with Harold?"

"Yes. His partner, Mr. Pearson, is still away, and he is doing all the work."

"Well done. He is sure to succeed. Where is Ida?"

"In her room, I think."

"She was with Charles Westmacott on the lawn not very long ago. He seems very fond of her. He is not very bright, but I think he will make her a good husband."

"I am sure of it, papa. He is very manly and reliable."

"Yes, I should think that he is not the sort of man who goes wrong. There is nothing hidden about him. As to his brightness, it really does not matter, for his aunt, Mrs. Westmacott, is very rich, much richer than you would think from her style of living, and she has made him a handsome provision."

"I am glad of that."

"It is between ourselves. I am her trustee, and so I know something of her arrangements. And when are you going to marry, Clara?"

"Oh, papa, not for some time yet. We have not thought of a date."

"Well, really, I don't know that there is any reason for delay. He has a competence and it increases yearly. As long as you are quite certain that your mind is made up——"

"Oh, papa!"

"Well, then, I really do not know why there should be any delay. And Ida, too, must be married within the next few months. Now, what I want to know is what I am to do when my two little companions run away from me." He spoke lightly, but his eyes were grave as he looked questioningly at his daughter.

"Dear papa, you shall not be alone. It will be years before Harold and I think of marrying, and when we do you must come and live with us."

"No, no, dear. I know that you mean what you say, but I have seen something of the world, and I know that such arrangements never answer. There cannot be two masters in a house, and yet at my age my freedom is very necessary to me."

"But you would be completely free."

"No, dear, you cannot be that if you are a guest in another man's house. Can you suggest no other alternative?"

"That we remain with you."

"No, no. That is out of the question. Mrs. Westmacott herself says that a woman's first duty is to marry. Marriage, however, should be an equal partnership, as she points out. I should wish you both to marry, but still I should like a suggestion from you, Clara, as to what *I* should do."

"But there is no hurry, papa. Let us wait. I do not intend to marry yet."

Doctor Walker looked disappointed. "Well, Clara, if you can suggest nothing, I suppose that I must take the initiative myself," said he.

"Then what do you propose, papa?" She braced herself as one who sees the blow which is about to fall.

He looked at her and hesitated. "How like your poor dear mother you are, Clara!" he cried. "As I looked at you then it was as if she had come back from the grave." He stooped towards her and kissed her. "There, run away to your sister, my dear, and do not trouble yourself about me. Nothing is settled yet, but you will find that all will come right."

Clara went upstairs sad at heart, for she was sure now that what she had feared was indeed about to come to pass, and that her father was going to take Mrs. Westmacott to be his wife. In her pure and earnest mind her mother's memory was enshrined as that of a saint, and the thought that any one should take her place seemed a terrible desecration. Even worse, however, did this marriage appear when looked at from the point of view of her father's future. The widow might fascinate him by her knowledge of the world, her dash, her strength, her unconventionality—all these qualities Clara was willing to allow her—but she was convinced that she would be unendurable as a life companion. She had come to an age when habits are not lightly to be changed, nor was she a woman who was at all likely to attempt to change them. How would a sensitive man like her father stand the constant strain of such a wife, a woman who was all decision, with no softness, and nothing soothing in her nature? It passed as a mere eccentricity when they heard of her stout drinking, her cigarette smoking, her occasional whiffs at a long clay pipe, her horsewhipping of a drunken servant, and her companionship with the snake Eliza, whom she was in the habit of bearing about in her pocket. All this would become unendurable to her father when his first infatuation was past. For his own sake, then, as well as for her mother's memory, this match must be prevented. And yet how powerless she was to prevent it! What could she do? Could Harold aid her? Perhaps. Or Ida? At least she could tell her sister and see what she could suggest.

Ida was in her boudoir, a tiny little tapestried room, as neat and dainty as herself, with low walls hung with Imari plaques and with pretty little Swiss brackets bearing blue Kaga ware, or the pure white Coalport china. In a low chair beneath a red shaded standing lamp sat Ida, in a diaphanous evening dress of *mousseline de soie,* the ruddy light tinging her sweet child-like face, and glowing on her golden curls. She sprang up as her sister entered, and threw her arms around her.

"Dear old Clara! Come and sit down here beside me. I have not had a chat for days. But, oh, what a troubled face! What is it then?" She put up her forefinger and smoothed her sister's brow with it.

Clara pulled up a stool, and sitting down beside her sister, passed her arm round her waist. "I am so sorry to trouble you, dear Ida," she said. "But I do not know what to do."

"There's nothing the matter with Harold?"

"Oh, no, Ida."

"Nor with my Charles?"

"No, no."

Ida gave a sigh of relief. "You quite frightened me, dear," said she. "You can't think how solemn you look. What is it, then?"

"I believe that papa intends to ask Mrs. Westmacott to marry him."

Ida burst out laughing. "What can have put such a notion into your head, Clara?"

"It is only too true, Ida. I suspected it before, and he himself almost told me as much with his own lips to-night. I don't think that it is a laughing matter."

"Really, I could not help it. If you had told me that those two dear old ladies opposite, the Misses Williams, were both engaged, you would not have surprised me more. It is really too funny."

"Funny, Ida! Think of any one taking the place of dear mother."

But her sister was of a more practical and less sentimental nature. "I am sure," said she, "that dear mother would like papa to do whatever would make him most happy. We shall both be away, and why should papa not please himself?"

"But think how unhappy he will be. You know how quiet he is in his ways, and how even a little thing will upset him. How could he live with a wife who would make his whole life a series of surprises? Fancy what a whirlwind she must be in a house. A man at his age cannot change his ways. I am sure he would be miserable."

Ida's face grew graver, and she pondered over the matter for a few minutes. "I really think that you are right as usual," said she at last. "I admire Charles's aunt very much, you know, and I think that she is a very useful and good person, but I don't think she would do as a wife for poor quiet papa."

"But he will certainly ask her, and I really think that she intends to accept him. Then it would be too late to interfere. We have only a few days at the most. And what can we do? How can we hope to make him change his mind?"

Again Ida pondered. "He has never tried what it is to live with a strong-minded woman," said she. "If we could only get him to realize it in time. Oh, Clara, I have it; I have it! Such a lovely plan!" She leaned back in her chair and burst into a fit of laughter so natural and so hearty that Clara had to forget her troubles and to join in it.

"Oh, it is beautiful!" she gasped at last. "Poor papa! What a time he will have! But it's all for his own good, as he used to say when we had to be punished when we were little. Oh, Clara, I do hope your heart won't fail you."

"I would do anything to save him, dear."

"That's it. You must steel yourself by that thought."

"But what is your plan?"

"Oh, I am so proud of it. We will tire him for ever of the widow, and of all emancipated women. Let me see, what are Mrs. Westmacott's main ideas? You have listened to her more than I. Women should attend less to household duties. That is one, is it not?"

"Yes, if they feel they have capabilities for higher things. Then she thinks that every woman who has leisure should take up the study of some branch of science, and that, as far as possible, every woman should qualify herself for some trade or profession, choosing for preference those which have been hitherto monopolized by men. To enter the others would only be to intensify the present competition."

"Quite so. That is glorious!" Her blue eyes were dancing with mischief, and she clapped her hands in delight. "What else? She thinks that whatever a man can do a woman should be allowed to do also—does she not?"

"She says so."

"And about dress? The short skirt, and the divided skirt are what she believes in?"

"Yes."

"We must get in some cloth."

"Why?"

"We must make ourselves a dress each. A brand-new, enfranchised, emancipated dress, dear. Don't you see my plan? We shall act up to all Mrs. Westmacott's views in every respect, and improve them when we can. Then papa will know what it is to live with a woman who claims all her rights. Oh, Clara, it will be splendid."

Her milder sister sat speechless before so daring a scheme. "But it would be wrong, Ida!" she cried at last.

"Not a bit. It is to save him."

"I should not dare."

"Oh, yes, you would. Harold will help. Besides, what other plan have you?"

"I have none."

"Then you must take mine."

"Yes. Perhaps you are right. Well, we do it for a good motive."

"You will do it?"

"I do not see any other way."

"You dear good Clara! Now I will show you what you are to do. We must not begin too suddenly. It might excite suspicion."

"What would you do, then?"

"To-morrow we must go to Mrs. Westmacott, and sit at her feet and learn all her views."

"What hypocrites we shall feel!"

"We shall be her newest and most enthusiastic converts. Oh, it will be such fun, Clara! Then we shall make our plans and send for what we want, and begin our new life."

"I do hope that we shall not have to keep it up long. It seems so cruel to dear papa."

"Cruel! To save him!"

"I wish I was sure that we were doing right. And yet what else can we do? Well, then, Ida, the die is cast, and we will call upon Mrs. Westmacott to-morrow."

All the morning the two girls sat extracting from Mrs. Westmacott her most extreme view.

9
A Family Plot

LITTLE did poor Doctor Walker imagine as he sat at his breakfast-table next morning that the two sweet girls who sat on either side of him were deep in a conspiracy, and that he, munching innocently at his muffins, was the victim against whom their wiles were planned. Patiently they waited until at last their opening came.

"It is a beautiful day," he remarked. "It will do for Mrs. Westmacott. She was thinking of having a spin upon the tricycle."

"Then we must call early. We both intended to see her after breakfast."

"Oh, indeed!" The Doctor looked pleased.

"You know, pa," said Ida, "it seems to us that we really have a very great advantage in having Mrs. Westmacott living so near."

"Why so, dear?"

"Well, because she is so advanced, you know. If we only study her ways we may advance ourselves also."

"I think I have heard you say, papa," Clara remarked, "that she is the type of the woman of the future."

"I am very pleased to hear you speak so sensibly, my dears. I certainly think that she is a woman whom you may very well take as your model. The more intimate you are with her the better pleased I shall be."

"Then that is settled," said Clara demurely, and the talk drifted to other matters.

All the morning the two girls sat extracting from Mrs. Westmacott her most extreme view as to the duty of the one sex and the tyranny of the other. Absolute equality, even in details, was her ideal. Enough of the parrot cry of unwomanly and unmaidenly. It had been invented by man to scare woman away when she poached too nearly upon his precious preserves. Every woman should be independent. Every woman should learn a trade. It was their duty to push in where they were least welcome. Then they were martyrs to the cause, and pioneers to their weaker sisters. Why should the wash-tub, the needle, and the housekeeper's book be eternally theirs? Might they not reach higher, to the consulting-room, to the bench, and even to the pulpit? Mrs. Westmacott sacrificed her tricycle ride in her eagerness over her pet subject, and her two fair disciples drank in every word, and noted every suggestion for future use. That afternoon they went shopping in London, and before evening strange packages began to be handed in at the Doctor's door. The plot was ripe for execution, and one of the conspirators was merry and jubilant, while the other was very nervous and troubled.

When the Doctor came down to the dining-room next morning, he was surprised to find that his daughters had already been up some time. Ida was installed at one end of the table with a spirit-lamp, a curved glass flask, and several bottles in front of her. The contents of the flask were boiling furiously, while a villainous smell filled the room. Clara lounged in an arm-chair with her feet upon a second one, a blue-covered book in her hand, and a huge map of the British Islands spread across her lap. "Hullo!" cried the Doctor, blinking and sniffing, "where's the breakfast?"

"Oh, didn't you order it?" asked Ida.

"I! No; why should I?" He rang the bell. "Why have you not laid the breakfast, Jane?"

"If you please, sir, Miss Ida was a workin' at the table."

"Oh, of course, Jane," said the young lady calmly. "I am so sorry. I shall be ready to move in a few minutes."

"But what on earth are you doing, Ida?" asked the Doctor. "The smell is most offensive. And, good gracious, look at the mess which you have made upon the cloth! Why, you have burned a hole right through."

"Oh, that is the acid," Ida answered contentedly. "Mrs. Westmacott said that it would burn holes."

"You might have taken her word for it without trying," said her father dryly.

"But look here, pa! See what the book says: 'The scientific mind takes nothing upon trust. Prove all things!' I have proved that."

"You certainly have. Well, until breakfast is ready I'll glance over *The Times*. Have you seen it?"

"*The Times?* Oh, dear me, this is it which I have under my spirit-lamp. I am afraid there is some acid upon that too, and it is rather damp and torn. Here it is."

The Doctor took the bedraggled paper with a rueful face. "Everything seems to be wrong to-day," he remarked. "What is this sudden enthusiasm about chemistry, Ida?"

"Oh, I am trying to live up to Mrs. Westmacott's teaching."

"Quite right! quite right!" said he, though perhaps

with less heartiness than he had shown the day before. "Ah, here is breakfast at last!"

But nothing was comfortable that morning. There were eggs without egg-spoons, toast which was leathery from being kept, dried-up rashers, and grounds in the coffee. Above all, there was that dreadful smell which pervaded everything and gave a horrible twang to every mouthful.

"I don't wish to put a damper upon your studies, Ida," said the Doctor, as he pushed back his chair. "But I do think it would be better if you did your chemical experiments a little later in the day."

"But Mrs. Westmacott says that women should rise early, and do their work before breakfast."

"Then they should choose some other room besides the breakfast-room." The Doctor was becoming just a little ruffled. A turn in the open air would soothe him, he thought. "Where are my boots?" he asked.

But they were not in their accustomed corner by his chair. Up and down he searched, while the three servants took up the quest, stooping and peeping under book-cases and drawers. Ida had returned to her studies, and Clara to her blue-covered volume, sitting absorbed and disinterested amid the bustle and the racket. At last a general buzz of congratulation announced that the cook had discovered the boots hung up among the hats in the hall. The Doctor, very red and flustered, drew them on, and stamped off to join the Admiral in his morning walk.

As the door slammed Ida burst into a shout of laughter. "You see, Clara," she cried, "the charm works already. He has gone to number one instead of to number three. Oh, we shall win a great victory.

You've been very good, dear; I could see that you were on thorns to help him when he was looking for his boots."

"Poor papa! It is so cruel. And yet what are we to do?"

"Oh, he will enjoy being comfortable all the more if we give him a little discomfort now. What horrible work this chemistry is! Look at my frock! It is ruined. And this dreadful smell!" She threw open the window, and thrust her little golden-curled head out of it. Charles Westmacott was hoeing at the other side of the garden fence.

"Good morning, sir," said Ida.

"Good morning!" The big man leaned upon his hoe and looked up at her.

"Have you any cigarettes, Charles?"

"Yes, certainly."

"Throw me up two."

"Here is my case. Can you catch?"

A seal-skin case came with a soft thud on to the floor. Ida opened it. It was full.

"What are these?" she asked.

"Egyptians."

"What are some other brands?"

"Oh, Richmond Gems, and Turkish, and Cambridge. But why?"

"Never mind!" She nodded to him and closed the window. "We must remember all those, Clara," said she. "We must learn to talk about such things. Mrs. Westmacott knows all about the brands of cigarettes. Has your rum come?"

"Yes, dear. It is here."

"And I have my stout. Come along up to my room

now. This smell is too abominable. But we must be ready for him when he comes back. If we sit at the window we shall see him coming down the road."

The fresh morning air, and the genial company of the Admiral had caused the Doctor to forget his troubles, and he came back about midday in an excellent humour. As he opened the hall door the vile smell of chemicals which had spoilt his breakfast met him with a redoubled virulence. He threw open the hall window, entered the dining-room, and stood aghast at the sight which met his eyes.

Ida was still sitting among her bottles, with a lit cigarette in her left hand and a glass of stout on the table beside her. Clara, with another cigarette, was lounging in the easy chair with several maps spread out upon the floor around. Her feet were stuck up on the coal scuttle, and she had a tumblerful of some reddish-brown composition on the smoking table close at her elbow. The Doctor gazed from one to the other of them through the thin grey haze of smoke, but his eyes rested finally in a settled stare of astonishment upon his elder and more serious daughter.

"Clara!" he gasped, "I could not have believed it!"

"What is it, papa?"

"You are smoking!"

"Trying to, papa. I find it a little difficult, for I have not been used to it."

"But why, in the name of goodness ——"

"Mrs. Westmacott recommends it."

"Oh, a lady of mature years may do many things which a young girl must avoid."

"Oh, no," cried Ida, "Mrs. Westmacott says that there should be one law for all. Have a cigarette, pa?"

"No, thank you. I never smoke in the morning."

"No? Perhaps you don't care for the brand. What are these, Clara?"

"Egyptians."

"Ah, we must have some Richmond Gems or Turkish. I wish, pa, when you go into town, you would get me some Turkish."

"I will do nothing of the kind. I do not at all think it is a fitting habit for young ladies. I do not agree with Mrs. Westmacott upon the point."

"Really, pa! It was you who advised us to imitate her."

"But with discrimination. What is it that you are drinking, Clara?"

"Rum, papa."

"Rum? In the morning?" He sat down and rubbed his eyes as one who tries to shake off some evil dream. "Did you say rum?"

"Yes, pa. They all drink it in the profession which I am going to take up."

"Profession, Clara?"

"Mrs. Westmacott says that every woman should follow a calling, and that we ought to choose those which women have always avoided."

"Quite so."

"Well, I am going to act upon her advice. I am going to be a pilot."

"My dear Clara! A pilot! This is too much."

"This is a beautiful book, papa. *The Lights, Beacons, Buoys, Channels, and Landmarks of Great Britain.* Here is another, *The Master Mariner's Handbook.* You can't imagine how interesting it is."

"You are joking, Clara. You must be joking!"

"Not at all, pa. You can't think what a lot I have learned already. I'm to carry a green light to starboard, and a red to port, with a white light at the mast-head, and a flare-up every fifteen minutes."

"Oh, won't it look pretty at night!" cried her sister.

"And I know the fog-signals. One blast means that a ship steers to starboard, two to port, three astern, four that it is unmanageable. But this man asks such dreadful questions at the end of each chapter. Listen to this: 'You see a red light. The ship is on the port tack and the wind at north; what course is that ship steering to a point?'"

The Doctor rose with a gesture of despair. "I can't imagine what has come over you both," said he.

"My dear papa, we are trying hard to live up to Mrs. Westmacott's standard."

"Well, I must say that I do not admire the result. Your chemistry, Ida, may perhaps do no harm; but your scheme, Clara, is out of the question. How a girl of your sense could ever entertain such a notion is more than I can imagine. But I must absolutely forbid you to go further with it."

"But, pa," asked Ida, with an air of innocent inquiry in her big blue eyes, "what are we to do when your commands and Mrs. Westmacott's advice are opposed? You told us to obey her. She says that when women try to throw off their shackles, their fathers, brothers, and husbands are the very first to try to rivet them on again, and that in such a matter no man has any authority."

"Does Mrs. Westmacott teach you that I am not the head of my own house?" The Doctor flushed, and his grizzled hair bristled in his anger.

"Certainly. She says that all heads of houses are relics of the dark ages."

The Doctor muttered something and stamped his foot upon the carpet. Then without a word he passed out into the garden and his daughters could see him striding furiously up and down, cutting off the heads of the flowers with a switch.

"Oh, you darling! You played your part so splendidly!" cried Ida.

"But how cruel it is! When I saw the sorrow and surprise in his eyes I very nearly put my arms about him and told him all. Don't you think we have done enough?"

"No, no, no. Not nearly enough. You must not turn weak now, Clara. It is so funny that I should be leading you. It is quite a new experience. But I know I am right. If we go on as we are going, we shall be able to say all our lives that we have saved him. And if we don't, oh, Clara, we should never forgive ourselves."

"Come in, papa! Do!"

10
Women of the Future

FROM that day the Doctor's peace was gone. Never was a quiet and orderly household transformed so suddenly into a bear garden, or a happy man turned into such a completely miserable one. He had never realized before how entirely his daughters had shielded him from all the friction of life. Now that they had not only ceased to protect him, but had themselves become a source of trouble to him, he began to understand how great the blessing was which he had enjoyed, and to sigh for the happy days before his girls had come under the influence of his neighbour.

"You don't look happy," Mrs. Westmacott had remarked to him one morning. "You are pale and a little off colour. You should come with me for a ten mile spin upon the tandem."

"I am troubled about my girls." They were walking up and down in the garden. From time to time there sounded from the house behind them the long, sad wail of a French horn.

"That is Ida," said he. "She has taken to practicing on that dreadful instrument in the intervals of her chemistry. And Clara is quite as bad. I declare it is getting quite unendurable."

"Ah, Doctor, Doctor!" she cried, shaking her forefinger, with a gleam of her white teeth. "You must live up to your principles—you must give your daughters the same liberty as you advocate for other women."

"Liberty, madam, certainly! But this approaches to license."

"The same law for all, my friend." She tapped him reprovingly on the arm with her sunshade. "When you were twenty your father did not, I presume, object to your learning chemistry or playing a musical instrument. You would have thought it tyranny if he had."

"But there is such a sudden change in them both."

"Yes, I have noticed that they have been very enthusiastic lately in the cause of liberty. Of all my disciples I think that they promise to be the most devoted and consistent, which is more natural since their father is one of our most trusted champions."

The Doctor gave a twitch of impatience. "I seem to have lost all authority," he cried.

"No, no, my dear friend. They are a little exuberant at having broken the trammels of custom. That is all."

"You cannot think what I have had to put up with, madam. It has been a dreadful experience. Last night, after I had extinguished the candle in my bedroom, I placed my foot upon something smooth and hard, which scuttled from under me. Imagine my horror! I lit the gas, and came upon a well-grown tortoise which Clara has thought fit to introduce into the house. I call it a filthy custom to have such pets."

Mrs. Westmacott dropped him a little courtesy. "Thank you, sir," said she. "That is a nice little side hit at my poor Eliza."

"I give you my word that I had forgotten about her," cried the Doctor, flushing. "One such pet may no doubt be endured, but two are more than I can bear. Ida has a monkey which lives on the curtain rod. It is a most dreadful creature. It will remain absolutely motionless until it sees that you have forgotten its presence, and then it will suddenly bound from picture to picture all round the walls, and end by swinging down on the bell-rope and jumping on to the top of your head. At breakfast it stole a poached egg and daubed it all over the door handle. Ida calls these outrages amusing tricks."

"Oh, all will come right," said the widow reassuringly.

"And Clara is as bad, Clara who used to be so good and sweet, the very image of her poor mother. She insists upon this preposterous scheme of being a pilot, and will talk of nothing but revolving lights and hidden rocks, and codes of signals, and nonsense of the kind."

"But why preposterous?" asked his companion. "What nobler occupation can there be than that of stimulating commerce, and aiding the mariner to steer safely into port? I should think your daughter admirably adapted for such duties."

"Then I must beg to differ from you, madam."

"Still, you are inconsistent."

"Excuse me, madam, I do not see the matter in the same light. And I should be obliged to you if you would use your influence with my daughter to dissuade her."

"You wish to make me inconsistent too."

"Then you refuse?"

"I am afraid that I cannot interfere."

The Doctor was very angry. "Very well, madam," said he. "In that case I can only say that I have the honour to wish you a very good morning." He raised his broad straw hat and strode away up the gravel path, while the widow looked after him with twinkling eyes. She was surprised herself to find that she liked the Doctor better the more masculine and aggressive he became. It was unreasonable and against all principle, and yet so it was and no argument could mend the matter.

Very hot and angry, the Doctor retired into his room and sat down to read his paper. Ida had retired, and the distant wails of the bugle showed that she was upstairs in her boudoir. Clara sat opposite to him with her exasperating charts and her blue book. The Doctor glanced at her and his eyes remained fixed in astonishment upon the front of her skirt.

"My dear Clara," he cried, "you have torn your skirt!"

His daughter laughed and smoothed out her frock. To his horror he saw the red plush of the chair where the dress ought to have been. "It is all torn!" he cried. "What have you done?"

"My dear papa!" said she, "what do you know about the mysteries of ladies' dress? This is a divided skirt."

Then he saw that it was indeed so arranged, and that his daughter was clad in a sort of loose, extremely long knickerbockers.

"It will be so convenient for my sea-boots," she explained.

Her father shook his head sadly. "Your dear mother would not have liked it, Clara," said he.

For a moment the conspiracy was upon the point of collapsing. There was something in the gentleness of his rebuke, and in his appeal to her mother, which brought the tears to her eyes, and in another instant she would have been kneeling beside him with everything confessed, when the door flew open and her sister Ida came bounding into the room. She wore a short grey skirt, like that of Mrs. Westmacott, and she held it up in each hand and danced about among the furniture.

"I feel quite the Gaiety girl!" she cried. "How delicious it must be to be upon the stage! You can't think how nice this dress is, papa. One feels so free in it. And isn't Clara charming?"

"Go to your room this instant and take it off!" thundered the Doctor. "I call it highly improper, and no daughter of mine shall wear it."

"Papa! Improper! Why, it is the exact model of Mrs. Westmacott's."

"I say it is improper. And yours also, Clara! Your conduct is really outrageous. You drive me out of the house. I am going to my club in town. I have no comfort or peace of mind in my own house. I will stand it no longer. I may be late to-night—I shall go to the British Medical meeting. But when I return I shall hope to find that you have reconsidered your conduct, and that you have shaken yourself clear of the pernicious influences which have recently made such an alteration in your conduct." He seized his hat, slammed the dining-room door, and a few minutes later they heard the crash of the big front gate.

"Victory, Clara, victory!" cried Ida, still pirouetting around the furniture. "Did you hear what he said? Pernicious influences! Don't you understand, Clara? Why do you sit there so pale and glum? Why don't you get up and dance?"

"Oh, I shall be so glad when it is over, Ida. I do hate to give him pain. Surely he has learned now that it is very unpleasant to spend one's life with reformers."

"He has almost learned it, Clara. Just one more little lesson. We must not risk all at this last moment."

"What would you do, Ida? Oh, don't do anything too dreadful. I feel that we have gone too far already."

"Oh, we can do it very nicely. You see we are both

engaged and that makes it very easy. Harold will do what you ask him, especially as you have told him the reason why, and my Charles will do it without even wanting to know the reason. Now you know what Mrs. Westmacott thinks about the reserve of young ladies. Mere prudery, affectation, and a relic of the dark ages of the Zenana. Those were her words, were they not?"

"What then?"

"Well, now we must put it in practice. We are reducing all her other views to practice, and we must not shirk this one."

"But what would you do? Oh, don't look so wicked, Ida! You look like some evil little fairy, with your golden hair and dancing, mischievous eyes. I know that you are going to propose something dreadful!"

"We must give a little supper to-night."

"We? A supper!"

"Why not? Young gentlemen give suppers. Why not young ladies?"

"But whom shall we invite?"

"Why, Harold and Charles of course."

"And the Admiral and Mrs. Hay Denver?"

"Oh, no. That would be very old-fashioned. We must keep up with the times, Clara."

"But what can we give them for supper?"

"Oh, something with a nice, fast, rollicking, late-at-night kind of flavor to it. Let me see! Champagne, of course—and oysters. Oysters will do. In the novels, all the naughty people take champagne and oysters. Besides, they won't need any cooking. How is your pocket-money, Clara?"

"I have three pounds."

"And I have one. Four pounds. I have no idea how much champagne costs. Have you?"

"Not the slightest."

"How many oysters does a man eat?"

"I can't imagine."

"I'll write and ask Charles. No, I won't. I'll ask Jane. Ring for her, Clara. She has been a cook, and is sure to know."

Jane, on being cross-questioned, refused to commit herself beyond the statement that it depended upon the gentleman, and also upon the oysters. The united experience of the kitchen, however, testified that three dozen was a fair provision.

"Then we shall have eight dozen altogether," said Ida, jotting down all her requirements upon a sheet of paper. "And two pints of champagne. And some brown bread, and vinegar, and pepper. That's all, I think. It is not so very difficult to give a supper after all, is it, Clara?"

"I don't like it, Ida. It seems to me to be so very indelicate."

"But it is needed to clinch the matter. No, no, there is no drawing back now, Clara, or we shall ruin everything. Papa is sure to come back by the 9:45. He will reach the door at 10. We must have everything ready for him. Now, just sit down at once, and ask Harold to come at nine o'clock, and I shall do the same to Charles."

The two invitations were dispatched, received and accepted. Harold was already a confidant, and he understood that this was some further development of the plot. As to Charles, he was so accustomed to feminine eccentricity, in the person of his aunt, that the only thing which could surprise him would be a rigid observance of etiquette. At nine o'clock they entered the dining-room of Number 2, to find the master of the house absent, a red-shaded lamp, a snowy cloth, a pleasant little feast, and the two whom they would have chosen, as their companions. A merrier party never met, and the house rang with their laughter and their chatter.

"It is three minutes to ten," cried Clara, suddenly, glancing at the clock.

"Good gracious! So it is! Now for our little tableau!" Ida pushed the champagne bottles obtrusively forward, in the direction of the door, and scattered oyster shells over the cloth.

"Have you your pipe, Charles?"

"My pipe! Yes."

"Then please smoke it. Now don't argue about it, but do it, for you will ruin the effect otherwise."

The large man drew out a red case, and extracted a great yellow meerschaum, out of which, a moment later, he was puffing thick wreaths of smoke. Harold had lit a cigar, and both the girls had cigarettes.

"That looks very nice and emancipated," said Ida, glancing round. "Now I shall lie on this sofa. So! Now, Charles, just sit here, and throw your arm carelessly over the back of the sofa. No, don't stop smoking. I like it. Clara, dear, put your feet upon the coal scuttle, and do try to look a little dissipated. I wish we could crown ourselves with flowers. There are some lettuces on the sideboard. Oh, dear, here he is! I hear his key." She began to sing in her high, fresh voice a little snatch from a French song, with a swinging tra-la-la chorus.

The Doctor had walked home from the station in a peaceful and relenting frame of mind, feeling that, perhaps, he had said too much in the morning, that his daughters had for years been models in every way, and that, if there had been any change of late, it was, as they said themselves, on account of their anxiety to follow his advice and to imitate Mrs. Westmacott. He could see clearly enough now that that advice was unwise, and that a world peopled with Mrs. Westmacotts would not be a happy or a soothing one. It was he who was, himself, to blame, and he was grieved by the thought that perhaps his hot words had troubled and saddened his two girls.

This fear, however, was soon dissipated. As he entered his hall he heard the voice of Ida uplifted in a rollicking ditty, and a very strong smell of tobacco was borne to his nostrils. He threw open the dining-room door, and stood aghast at the scene which met his eyes.

The room was full of the blue wreaths of smoke, and the lamp-light shone through the thin haze upon gold-topped bottles, plates, napkins, and a litter of oyster shells and cigarettes. Ida, flushed and excited, was reclining upon the settee, a wine-glass at her elbow, and a cigarette between her fingers, while Charles Westmacott sat beside her, with his arm thrown over the head of the sofa, with the suggestion of a caress. On the other side of the room, Clara was lounging in an arm-chair, with Harold beside her, both smoking, and both with wine-glasses beside them. The Doctor stood speechless in the doorway, staring at the Bacchanalian scene.

"Come in, papa! Do!" cried Ida. "Won't you have a glass of champagne?"

"Pray excuse me," said her father, coldly, "I feel that I am intruding. I did not know that you were entertaining. Perhaps you will kindly let me know when you have finished. You will find me in my study." He ignored the two young men completely, and, closing the door, retired, deeply hurt and mortified, to his room. A quarter of an hour afterwards he heard the door slam, and his two daughters came to announce that the guests were gone.

"Guests! Whose guests?" he cried angrily. "What is the meaning of this exhibition?"

"We have been giving a little supper, papa. They were our guests."

"Oh, indeed!" The Doctor laughed sarcastically. "You think it right, then, to entertain young bachelors late at night, to smoke and drink with them, to— Oh, that I should ever have lived to blush for my own daughters! I thank God that your dear mother never saw the day."

"Dearest papa," cried Clara, throwing her arms about him. "Do not be angry with us. If you understood all, you would see that there is no harm in it."

"No harm, miss! Who is the best judge of that?"

"Mrs. Westmacott," suggested Ida, slyly.

The Doctor sprang from his chair. "Confound Mrs. Westmacott!" he cried, striking frenziedly into the air with his hands. "Am I to hear of nothing but this woman? Is she to confront me at every turn? I will endure it no longer."

"But it was your wish, papa."

"Then I will tell you now what my second and wiser wish is, and we shall see if you will obey it as you have the first."

"Of course we will, papa."

"Then my wish is, that you should forget these odious notions which you have imbibed, that you should dress and act as you used to do, before ever you saw this woman, and that, in future, you confine your intercourse with her to such civilities as are necessary between neighbours."

"We are to give up Mrs. Westmacott?"

"Or give up me."

"Oh, dear dad, how can you say anything so cruel?" cried Ida, burrowing her towsy golden hair into her father's shirt front, while Clara pressed her cheek against his whisker. "Of course we shall give her up, if you prefer it."

"Of course we shall, papa."

The Doctor patted the two caressing heads. "These are my own two girls again," he cried. "It has been my fault as much as yours. I have been astray, and you have followed me in my error. It was only by seeing your mistake that I have become conscious of my own. Let us set it aside, and neither say nor think anything more about it."

"I am ruined, mother—ruined!"

11
A Bolt from the Blue

So by the cleverness of two girls a dark cloud was thinned away and turned into sunshine. Over one of them, alas, another cloud was gathering, which could not be so easily dispersed. Of these three households which fate had thrown together, two had already been united by ties of love. It was destined, however, that a bond of another sort should connect the Westmacotts with the Hay Denvers.

Between the Admiral and the widow a very cordial feeling had existed since the day when the old seaman had hauled down his flag and changed his opinions; granting to the yachtswoman all that he had refused to the reformer. His own frank and downright nature respected the same qualities in his neighbour, and a friendship sprang up between them which was more like that which exists between two men, founded upon esteem and a community of tastes.

"By the way, Admiral," said Mrs. Westmacott one morning, as they walked together down to the station, "I understand that this boy of yours in the intervals of paying his devotions to Miss Walker is doing something upon 'Change."

"Yes, ma'am, and there is no man of his age who is doing so well. He's drawing ahead, I can tell you, ma'am. Some of those that started with him are hull down astarn now. He touched his five hundred last year, and before he's thirty he'll be making the four figures."

"The reason I asked is that I have small investments to make myself from time to time, and my present broker is a rascal. I should be very glad to do it through your son."

"It is very kind of you, ma'am. His partner is away on a holiday, and Harold would like to push on a bit and show what he can do. You know the poop isn't big enough to hold the lieutenant when the skipper's on shore."

"I suppose he charges the usual half per cent?"

"Don't know, I'm sure, ma'am. I'll swear that he does what is right and proper."

"That is what I usually pay—ten shillings in the hundred pounds. If you see him before I do just ask him to get me five thousand in New Zealands. It is at four just now, and I fancy it may rise."

"Five thousand!" exclaimed the Admiral, reckoning it in his own mind. "Lemme see! That's twenty-five pounds commission. A nice day's work, upon my word. It is a very handsome order, ma'am."

"Well, I must pay some one, and why not him?"

"I'll tell him, and I'm sure he'll lose no time."

"Oh, there is no great hurry. By the way, I understand from what you said just now that he has a partner."

"Yes, my boy is the junior partner. Pearson is the senior. I was introduced to him years ago, and he offered Harold the opening. Of course we had a pretty stiff premium to pay."

Mrs. Westmacott had stopped, and was standing

very stiffly with her Red Indian face even grimmer than usual.

"Pearson?" said she. "Jeremiah Pearson?"

"The same."

"Then it's all off," she cried. "You need not carry out that investment."

"Very well, ma'am."

They walked on together side by side, she brooding over some thought of her own, and he a little crossed and disappointed at her caprice and the lost commission for Harold.

"I tell you what, Admiral," she exclaimed suddenly, "if I were you I should get your boy out of this partnership."

"But why, madam?"

"Because he is tied to one of the deepest, slyest foxes in the whole city of London."

"Jeremiah Pearson, ma'am? What can you know of him? He bears a good name."

"No one in the world knows Jeremiah Pearson as I know him, Admiral. I warn you because I have a friendly feeling both for you and for your son. The man is a rogue and you had best avoid him."

"But these are only words, ma'am. Do you tell me that you know him better than the brokers and jobbers in the City?"

"Man," cried Mrs. Westmacott, "will you allow that I know him when I tell you that my maiden name was Ada Pearson, and that Jeremiah is my only brother?"

The Admiral whistled. "Whew!" cried he. "Now that I think of it, there is a likeness."

"He is a man of iron, Admiral—a man without a heart. I should shock you if I were to tell you what I have endured from my brother. My father's wealth was divided equally between us. His own share he ran through in five years, and he has tried since then by every trick of a cunning, low-minded man, by base cajolery, by legal quibbles, by brutal intimidation, to juggle me out of my share as well. There is no villainy of which the man is not capable. Oh, I know my brother Jeremiah. I know him and I am prepared for him."

"This is all new to me, ma'am. 'Pon my word, I hardly know what to say to it. I thank you for having spoken so plainly. From what you say, this is a poor sort of consort for a man to sail with. Perhaps Harold would do well to cut himself adrift."

"Without losing a day."

"Well, we shall talk it over. You may be sure of that. But here we are at the station, so I will just see you into your carriage and then home to see what my wife says to the matter."

As he trudged homewards, thoughtful and perplexed, he was surprised to hear a shout behind him, and to see Harold running down the road after him.

"Why, dad," he cried, "I have just come from town, and the first thing I saw was your back as you marched away. But you are such a quick walker that I had to run to catch you."

The Admiral's smile of pleasure had broken his stern face into a thousand wrinkles. "You are early to-day," said he.

"Yes, I wanted to consult you."

"Nothing wrong?"

"Oh, no, only an inconvenience."

"What is it, then?"

"How much have we in our private account?"

"Pretty fair. Some eight hundred, I think."

"Oh, half that will be ample. It was rather thoughtless of Pearson."

"What, then?"

"Well, you see, dad, when he went away upon this little holiday to Havre he left me to pay accounts and so on. He told me that there was enough at the bank for all claims. I had occasion on Tuesday to pay away two cheques, one for £80, and the other for £120, and here they are returned with a bank notice that we have already overdrawn to the extent of some hundreds."

The Admiral looked very grave. "What's the meaning of that, then?" he asked.

"Oh, it can easily be set right. You see Pearson invests all the spare capital and keeps as small a margin as possible at the bank. Still it was too bad for him to allow me even to run a risk of having a cheque returned. I have written to him and demanded his authority to sell out some stock, and I have written an explanation to these people. In the meantime, however, I have had to issue several cheques; so I had better transfer part of our private account to meet them."

"Quite so, my boy. All that's mine is yours. But who do you think this Pearson is? He is Mrs. Westmacott's brother."

"Really. What a singular thing! Well, I can see a likeness now that you mention it. They have both the same hard type of face."

"She has been warning me against him—says he is the rankest pirate in London. I hope that it is all right, boy, and that we may not find ourselves in broken water."

Harold had turned a little pale as he heard Mrs. Westmacott's opinion of his senior partner. It gave shape and substance to certain vague fears and suspicions of his own which had been pushed back as often as they obtruded themselves as being too monstrous and fantastic for belief.

"He is a well-known man in the City, dad," said he.

"Of course he is—of course he is. That is what I told her. They would have found him out there if anything had been amiss with him. Bless you, there's nothing so bitter as a family quarrel. Still it is just as well that you have written about this affair, for we may as well have all fair and aboveboard."

But Harold's letter to his partner was crossed by a letter from his partner to Harold. It lay awaiting him upon the breakfast table next morning, and it sent the heart into his mouth as he read it, and caused him to spring up from his chair with a white face and staring eyes.

"My boy! My boy!"

"I am ruined, mother—ruined!" He stood gazing wildly in front of him, while the sheet of paper fluttered down on the carpet. Then he dropped back into the chair, and sank his face into his hands. His mother had her arms round him in an instant, while the Admiral, with shaking fingers, picked up the letter from the floor and adjusted his glasses to read it.

"MY DEAR DENVER," it ran. "By the time that this reaches you I shall be out of the reach of yourself or of any one else who may desire an interview. You need not search for me, for I assure you that this letter is posted by a friend, and that you will have your trouble in vain if you try to find me. I am sorry to leave you in such a tight place, but one or other of us must be squeezed, and on the whole I prefer that it should be you. You'll find nothing in the bank, and about £13,000 unaccounted for. I'm not sure that the best thing you can do is not to realize what you can, and imitate your senior's example. If you act at once you may get clean away. If not, it's not only that you must put up your shutters, but I am afraid that this missing money could hardly be included as an ordinary debt, and of course you are legally responsible for it just as much as I am. Take a friend's advice and get to America. A young man with brains can always do something out there, and you can live down this little mischance. It will be a cheap lesson if it teaches you to take nothing upon trust in business, and to insist upon knowing exactly what your partner is doing, however senior he may be to you.

"Yours faithfully,

"JEREMIAH PEARSON."

"Great Heavens!" groaned the Admiral, "he has absconded."

"And left me both a bankrupt and a thief."

"No, no, Harold," sobbed his mother. "All will be right. What matter about money!"

"Money, mother! It is my honour."

"The boy is right. It is his honour, and my honour, for his is mine. This is a sore trouble, mother, when we thought our life's troubles were all behind us, but we will bear it as we have borne others." He held out his stringy hand, and the two old folk sat with bowed grey heads, their fingers intertwined, strong in each other's love and sympathy.

"We were too happy," she sighed.

"But it is God's will, mother."

"Yes, John, it is God's will."

"And yet it is bitter to bear. I could have lost all, the

house, money, rank—I could have borne it. But at my age—my honour—the honour of an admiral of the fleet."

"No honour can be lost, John, where no dishonour has been done. What have you done? What has Harold done? There is no question of honour."

The old man shook his head, but Harold had already called together his clear practical sense, which for an instant in the presence of this frightful blow had deserted him.

"The matter is right, dad," said he. "It is bad enough, Heaven knows, but we must not take too dark a view of it. After all, this insolent letter is in itself evidence that I had nothing to do with the schemes of the base villain who wrote it."

"They may think it prearranged."

"They could not. My whole life cries out against the thought. They could not look me in the face and entertain it."

"No, boy, not if they have eyes in their heads," cried the Admiral, plucking up courage at the sight of the flashing eyes and brave, defiant face. "We have the letter, and we have your character. We'll weather it yet between them. It's my fault from the beginning for choosing such a land-shark for your consort. God help me, I thought I was finding such an opening for you."

"Dear dad! How could you possibly know? As he says in his letter, it has given me a lesson. But he was so much older and so much more experienced, that it was hard for me to ask to examine his books. But we must waste no time. I must go to the City."

"What will you do?"

"What an honest man should do. I will write to all our clients and creditors, assemble them, lay the whole matter before them, read them the letter and put myself absolutely in their hands."

"That's it, boy—yard-arm to yard-arm, and have it over."

"I must go at once." He put on his top-coat and his hat. "But I have ten minutes yet before I can catch a train. There is one little thing which I must do before I start."

He had caught sight through the long glass folding door of the gleam of a white blouse and a straw hat in the tennis ground. Clara used often to meet him there of a morning to say a few words before he hurried away into the City. He walked out now with the quick, firm step of a man who has taken a momentous resolution, but his face was haggard and his lips pale.

"Clara," said he, as she came towards him with words of greeting, "I am sorry to bring ill news to you, but things have gone wrong in the City, and—and I think that I ought to release you from your engagement."

Clara stared at him with her great questioning dark eyes, and her face became as pale as his.

"How can the City affect you and me, Harold?"

"It is dishonour. I cannot ask you to share it."

"Dishonour! The loss of some miserable gold and silver coins!"

"Oh, Clara, if it were only that! We could be far happier together in a little cottage in the country than with all the riches of the City. Poverty could not cut me to the heart, as I have been cut this morning. Why, it is but twenty minutes since I had the letter, Clara, and it seems to me to be some old, old thing which happened far away in my past life, some horrid black cloud which shut out all the freshness and the peace from it."

"But what is it, then? What do you fear worse than poverty?"

"To have debts that I cannot meet. To be hammered upon 'Change and declared a bankrupt. To know that others have a just claim upon me and to feel that I dare not meet their eyes. Is not that worse than poverty?"

"Yes, Harold, a thousand fold worse! But all this may be got over. Is there nothing more?"

"My partner has fled and left me responsible for heavy debts, and in such a position that I may be required by the law to produce some at least of this missing money. It has been confided to him to invest, and he has embezzled it. I, as his partner, am liable for it. I have brought misery on all whom I love—my father, my mother. But you at least shall not be under the shadow. You are free, Clara. There is no tie between us."

"It takes two to make such a tie, Harold," said she, smiling and putting her hand inside his arm. "It takes two to make it, dear, and also two to break it. Is that the way they do business in the City, sir, that a man can always at his own sweet will tear up his engagement?"

"You hold me to it, Clara?"

"No creditor so remorseless as I, Harold. Never, never shall you get from that bond."

"But I am ruined. My whole life is blasted."

"And so you wish to ruin me, and blast my life also. No indeed, sir, you shall not get away so lightly. But seriously now, Harold, you would hurt me if it were not so absurd. Do you think that a woman's love is like this sunshade which I carry in my hand, a thing only fitted for the sunshine, and of no use when the winds blow and the clouds gather?"

"I would not drag you down, Clara."

"Should I not be dragged down indeed if I left your side at such a time? It is only now that I can be of use to you, help you, sustain you. You have always been so strong, so above me. You are strong still, but then two will be stronger. Besides, sir, you have no idea what a woman of business I am. Papa says so, and he knows."

Harold tried to speak, but his heart was too full. He could only press the white hand which curled round his sleeve. She walked up and down by his side, prattling merrily, and sending little gleams of cheeriness through the gloom which girt him in. To listen to her he might have thought that it was Ida, and not her staid and demure sister, who was chatting to him.

"It will soon be cleared up," she said, "and then we shall feel quite dull. Of course all business men have these little ups and downs. Why, I suppose of all the men you meet upon 'Change, there is not one who has not some such story to tell. If everything was always smooth, you know, then of course every one would turn stockbroker, and you would have to hold your meetings in Hyde Park. How much is it that you need?"

"More than I can ever get. Not less than thirteen thousand pounds."

Clara's face fell as she heard the amount. "What do you purpose doing?"

"I shall go to the City now, and I shall ask all our creditors to meet me to-morrow. I shall read them Pearson's letter, and put myself into their hands."

"And they, what will they do?"

"What can they do? They will serve writs for their money, and the firm will be declared bankrupt."

"And the meeting will be to-morrow, you say. Will you take my advice?"

"What is it, Clara?"

"To ask them for a few days of delay. Who knows what new turn matters may take?"

"What turn can they take? I have no means of raising the money."

"Let us have a few days."

"Oh, we should have that in the ordinary course of business. The legal formalities would take them some little time. But I must go, Clara, I must not seem to shirk. My place now must be at my offices."

"Yes, dear, you are right. God bless you and guard you! I shall be here in The Wilderness, but all day I shall be by your office table at Throgmorton Street in spirit, and if ever you should be sad you will hear my little whisper in your ear, and know that there is one client whom you will never be able to get rid of—never as long as we both live, dear."

12
Friends in Need

"NOW, PAPA," said Clara that morning, wrinkling her brows and putting her finger-tips together with the air of an experienced person of business. "I want to have a talk to you about money matters."

"Yes, my dear." He laid down his paper, and looked a question.

"Kindly tell me again, papa, how much money I have in my very own right. You have often told me before, but I always forget figures."

"You have two hundred and fifty pounds a year of your own, under your aunt's will."

"And Ida?"

"Ida has one hundred and fifty."

"Now, I think I can live very well on fifty pounds a year, papa. I am not very extravagant, and I could make my own dresses if I had a sewing-machine."

"Very likely, dear."

"In that case I have two hundred a year which I could do without."

"If it were necessary."

"But it is necessary. Oh, do help me, like a good, dear, kind papa, in this matter, for my whole heart is set upon it. Harold is in sore need of money, and through no fault of his own." With a woman's tact and eloquence, she told the whole story. "Put yourself in my place, papa. What is the money to me? I never think of it from year's end to year's end. But now I know how precious it is. I could not have thought that money could be so valuable. See what I can do with it. It may help to save him. I must have it by to-morrow. Oh, do, do advise me as to what I should do, and how I should get the money."

The Doctor smiled at her eagerness. "You are as anxious to get rid of money as others are to gain it," said he. "In another case I might think it rash, but I believe in your Harold, and I can see that he has had villainous treatment. You will let me deal with the matter."

"You, papa?"

"It can be done best between men. Your capital, Clara, is some five thousand pounds, but it is out on a mortgage, and you could not call it in."

"Oh, dear! oh, dear!"

"But we can still manage. I have as much at my bank. I will advance it to the Denvers as coming from you, and you can repay it to me, or the interest of it, when your money becomes due."

"Oh, that is beautiful! How sweet and kind of you!"

"But there is one obstacle: I do not think that you would ever induce Harold to take this money."

Clara's face fell. "Don't you think so, really?"

"I am sure that he would not."

"Then what are you to do? What horrid things money matters are to arrange!"

"I shall see his father. We can manage it all between us."

"Oh, do, do, papa! And you will do it soon?"

"There is no time like the present. I will go in at once." He scribbled a cheque, put it in an envelope, put on his broad straw hat, and strolled in through the garden to pay his morning call.

It was a singular sight which met his eyes as he entered the sitting-room of the Admiral. A great sea chest stood open in the centre, and all round upon the carpet were little piles of jerseys, oil-skins, books, sextant boxes, instruments, and sea-boots. The old seaman sat gravely amidst this lumber, turning it over, and examining it intently; while his wife, with the tears running silently down her ruddy cheeks, sat upon the sofa, her elbows upon her knees and her chin upon her hands, rocking herself slowly backwards and forwards.

"Hullo, Doctor," said the Admiral, holding out his hand, "there's foul weather set in upon us, as you may have heard, but I have ridden out many a worse squall, and, please God, we shall all three of us weather this one also, though two of us are a little more cranky than we were."

"My dear friends, I came in to tell you how deeply we sympathize with you all. My girl has only just told me about it."

"It has come so suddenly upon us, Doctor," sobbed Mrs. Hay Denver. "I thought that I had John to myself for the rest of our lives—Heaven knows that we have not seen very much of each other—but now he talks of going to sea again."

"Aye, aye, Walker, that's the only way out of it. When I first heard of it I was thrown up in the wind with all aback. I give you my word that I lost my bearings more completely than ever since I strapped a middy's dirk to my belt. You see, friend, I know something of shipwreck or battle or whatever may come upon the waters, but the shoals in the City of London on which my poor boy has struck are clean beyond me. Pearson had been my pilot there, and now I know him to be a rogue. But I've taken my bearings now, and I see my course right before me."

"What then, Admiral?"

"Oh, I have one or two little plans. I'll have some news for the boy. Why, hang it, Walker, man, I may be a bit stiff in the joints, but you'll be my witness that I can do my twelve miles under the three hours. What then? My eyes are as good as ever except just for the newspaper. My head is clear. I'm three-and-sixty, but I'm as good a man as ever I was—too good a man to lie up for another ten years. I'd be the better for a smack of the salt water again, and a whiff of the breeze. Tut, mother, it's not a four years' cruise this time. I'll be back every month or two. It's no more than if I went for a visit in the country." He was talking boisterously, and heaping his sea-boots and sextants back into his chest.

"And you really think, my dear friend, of hoisting your pennant again?"

"My pennant, Walker? No, no. Her Majesty, God bless her, has too many young men to need an old hulk like me. I should be plain Mr. Hay Denver, of the merchant service. I daresay that I might find some owner who would give me a chance as second or third officer. It will be strange to me to feel the rails of the bridge under my fingers once more."

"Tut! tut! this will never do, this will never do, Admiral!" The Doctor sat down by Mrs. Hay Denver and patted her hand in token of friendly sympathy. "We must wait until your son has had it out with all these people, and then we shall know what damage is done, and how best to set it right. It will be time enough then to begin to muster our resources to meet it."

"Our resources!" The Admiral laughed. "There's the pension. I'm afraid, Walker, that our resources won't need much mustering."

"Oh, come, there are some which you may not have thought of. For example, Admiral, I had always intended that my girl should have five thousand from me when she married. Of course, your boy's trouble is her trouble, and the money cannot be spent better than in helping to set it right. She has a little of her own which she wished to contribute, but I thought it best to work it this way. Will you take the cheque, Mrs. Denver, and I think it would be best if you said nothing to Harold about it, and just used it as the occasion served?"

"God bless you, Walker, you are a true friend. I won't forget this, Walker." The Admiral sat down on his sea chest and mopped his brow with his red handkerchief.

"What is it to me whether you have it now or then? It may be more useful now. There's only one stipulation. If things should come to the worst, and if the business should prove so bad that nothing can set it right, then hold back this cheque, for there is no use in pouring water into a broken basin, and if the lad should fall, he will want something to pick himself up again with."

"He shall not fall, Walker, and you shall not have occasion to be ashamed of the family into which your daughter is about to marry. I have my own plan. But we shall hold your money, my friend, and it will strengthen us to feel that it is there."

"Well, that is all right," said Doctor Walker, rising. "And if a little more should be needed, we must not let him go wrong for the want of a thousand or two. And now, Admiral, I'm off for my morning walk. Won't you come too?"

"No, I am going into town."

"Well, good-bye. I hope to have better news, and that all will come right. Good-bye, Mrs. Denver. I feel as if the boy were my own, and I shall not be easy until all is right with him."

13
In Strange Waters

WHEN Doctor Walker had departed, the Admiral packed all his possessions back into his sea chest with the exception of one little brass-bound desk. This he unlocked, and took from it a dozen or so blue sheets of paper all mottled over with stamps and seals, with very large V.R.'s printed upon the heads of them. He tied these carefully into a small bundle, and placing them in the inner pocket of his coat, he seized his stick and hat.

"Oh, John, don't do this rash thing," cried Mrs. Denver, laying her hands upon his sleeve. "I have seen so little of you, John. Only three years since you left the service. Don't leave me again. I know it is weak of me, but I cannot bear it."

"There's my own brave lass," said he, smoothing down the grey-shot hair. "We've lived in honour together, mother, and please God in honour we'll die. No matter how debts are made, they have got to be met, and what the boy owes we owe. He has not the money, and how is he to find it? He can't find it. What then? It becomes my business, and there's only one way for it."

"But it may not be so very bad, John. Had we not best wait until after he sees these people to-morrow?"

"They may give him little time, lass. But I'll have a care that I don't go so far that I can't put back again.

Now, mother, there's no use holding me. It's got to be done, and there's no sense in shirking it." He detached her fingers from his sleeve, pushed her gently back into an arm-chair, and hurried from the house.

In less than half an hour the Admiral was whirled into Victoria Station and found himself amid a dense bustling throng, who jostled and pushed in the crowded terminus. His errand, which had seemed feasible enough in his own room, began now to present difficulties in the carrying out, and he puzzled over how he should take the first steps. Amid the stream of business men, each hurrying on his definite way, the old seaman in his grey tweed suit and black soft hat strode slowly along, his head sunk and his brow wrinkled in perplexity. Suddenly an idea occurred to him. He walked back to the railway stall and bought a daily paper. This he turned and turned until a certain column met his eye, when he smoothed it out, and carrying it over to a seat, proceeded to read it at his leisure.

And, indeed, as a man read that column, it seemed strange to him that there should still remain any one in this world of ours who should be in straits for want of money. Here were whole lines of gentlemen who were burdened with a surplus in their incomes, and who were loudly calling to the poor and needy to come and take it off their hands. Here was the guileless person who was not a professional moneylender, but who would be glad to correspond, etc. Here too was the accommodating individual who advanced sums from ten to ten thousand pounds without expense, security, or delay. "The money actually paid over within a few hours," ran this fascinating advertisement, conjuring up a vision of swift messengers rushing with bags of gold to the aid of the poor struggler. A third gentleman did all business by personal application, advanced money on anything or nothing; the lightest and airiest promise was enough to content him according to his circular, and finally he never asked for more than five per cent. This struck the Admiral as far the most promising, and his wrinkles relaxed, and his frown softened away as he gazed at it. He folded up the paper, rose from the seat, and found himself face to face with Charles Westmacott.

"Hullo, Admiral!"

"Hullo, Westmacott!" Charles had always been a favourite of the seaman's. "What are you doing here?"

"Oh, I have been doing a little business for my aunt. But I have never seen you in London before."

"I hate the place. It smothers me. There's not a breath of clean air on this side of Greenwich. But maybe you know your way about pretty well in the City?"

"Well, I know something about it. You see I've never lived very far from it, and I do a good deal of my aunt's business."

"Maybe you know Bread Street?"

"It is out of Cheapside."

"Well then, how do you steer for it from here? You make me out a course and I'll keep to it."

"Why, Admiral, I have nothing to do. I'll take you there with pleasure."

"Will you, though? Well, I'd take it very kindly if you would. I have business there. Smith and Hanbury, financial agents, Bread Street."

The pair made their way to the river-side, and so down the Thames to St. Paul's landing—a mode of travel which was much more to the Admiral's taste than 'bus or cab. On the way, he told his companion his mission and the causes which had led to it. Charles Westmacott knew little enough of City life and the ways of business, but at least he had more experience in both than the Admiral, and he made up his mind not to leave him until the matter was settled.

"These are the people," said the Admiral, twisting round his paper, and pointing to the advertisement which had seemed to him the most promising. "It sounds honest and aboveboard, does it not? The personal interview looks as if there were no trickery, and then no one could object to five per cent."

"No, it seems fair enough."

"It is not pleasant to have to go hat in hand borrowing money, but there are times, as you may find before you are my age, Westmacott, when a man must stow away his pride. But here's their number, and their plate is on the corner of the door."

A narrow entrance was flanked on either side by a row of brasses, ranging upwards from the shipbrokers and the solicitors who occupied the ground floors, through a long succession of West Indian agents, architects, surveyors, and brokers, to the firm of which they were in quest. A winding stone stair, well carpeted and railed at first, but growing shabbier with every landing, brought them past innumerable doors until, at last, just under the ground-glass roofing, the names of Smith and Hanbury were to be seen painted in large white letters across a panel, with a laconic invitation to push beneath it. Following out the suggestion, the Admiral and his companion found themselves in a dingy apartment, ill lit from a couple of glazed windows. An ink-stained table, littered with pens, papers, and almanacs, an American cloth sofa, three chairs of varying patterns, and a much-worn carpet, constituted all the furniture, save only a very large and obtrusive porcelain spittoon, and a gaudily framed and very sombre picture which hung above the fireplace. Sitting in front of this picture, and staring gloomily at it, as being the only thing which he could stare at, was a small sallow-faced boy with a large head, who in the intervals of his art studies munched sedately at an apple.

"Is Mr. Smith or Mr. Hanbury in?" asked the Admiral.

"There ain't no such people," said the small boy.

"But you have the names on the door."

"Ah, that is the name of the firm, you see. It's only a name. It's Mr. Reuben Metaxa that you wants."

"Well, then, is he in?"

"No, he's not."

"When will he be back?"

"Can't tell, I'm sure. He's gone to lunch. Sometimes he takes one hour, and sometimes two. It'll be two to-day, I 'spect, for he said he was hungry afore he went."

"Then I suppose that we had better call again," said the Admiral.

"Not a bit," cried Charles. "I know how to manage these little imps. See here, you young varmint, here's a shilling for you. Run off and fetch your master. If you don't bring him here in five minutes I'll clump you on the side of the head when you get back. Shoo! Scat!" He charged at the youth, who bolted from the room and clattered madly down-stairs.

"He'll fetch him," said Charles. "Let us make ourselves at home. This sofa does not feel over and above safe. It was not meant for fifteen-stone men. But this doesn't look quite the sort of place where one would expect to pick up money."

"Just what I was thinking," said the Admiral, looking ruefully about him.

"Ah, well! I have heard that the best furnished offices generally belong to the poorest firms. Let us hope it's the opposite here. They can't spend much on the management, anyhow. That pumpkin-headed boy was the staff, I suppose. Ha, by Jove, that's his voice, and he's got our man, I think!"

As he spoke the youth appeared in the doorway with a small, brown, dried-up little chip of a man at his heels. He was clean-shaven and blue-chinned, with bristling black hair, and keen brown eyes which shone our very brightly from between pouched under-lids and drooping upper ones. He advanced, glancing keenly from one to the other of his visitors, and slowly rubbing together his thin, blue-veined hands. The small boy closed the door behind him, and discreetly vanished.

"I am Mr. Reuben Metaxa," said the moneylender. "Was it about an advance you wished to see me?"

"Yes."

"For you, I presume?" turning to Charles Westmacott.

"No, for this gentleman."

The moneylender looked surprised. "How much did you desire?"

"I thought of five thousand pounds," said the Admiral.

"And on what security?"

"I am a retired admiral of the British Navy. You will find my name in the Navy List. There is my card. I have here my pension papers. I get £850 a year. I thought that perhaps if you were to hold these papers it would be security enough that I should repay you. You could draw my pension, and repay yourselves at the rate, say, of £500 a year, taking your five per cent. interest as well."

"What interest?"

"Five per cent. per annum."

Mr. Metaxa laughed. "Per annum!" he said. "Five per cent. a month."

"A month! That would be sixty per cent. a year."

"Precisely."

"But that is monstrous."

"I don't ask gentlemen to come to me. They come of their own free will. Those are my terms, and they can take it or leave it."

"Then I shall leave it." The Admiral rose angrily from his chair.

"But one moment, sir. Just sit down and we shall chat the matter over. Yours is a rather unusual case and we may find some other way of doing what you wish. Of course the security which you offer is no security at all, and no sane man would advance five thousand pennies on it."

"No security? Why not, sir?"

"You might die to-morrow. You are not a young man. What age are you?"

"Sixty-three."

Mr. Metaxa turned over a long column of figures. "Here is an actuary's table," said he. "At your time of life the average expectancy of life is only a few years even in a well-preserved man."

"Do you mean to insinuate that I am not a well-preserved man?"

"Well, Admiral, it is a trying life at sea. Sailors in their younger days are gay dogs, and take it out of themselves. Then when they grow older they are still hard at it, and have no chance of rest or peace. I do not think a sailor's life a good one."

"I'll tell you what, sir," said the Admiral hotly. "If you have two pairs of gloves I'll undertake to knock you out under three rounds. Or I'll race you from here to St. Paul's, and my friend here will see fair. I'll let you see whether I am an old man or not."

"This is beside the question," said the moneylender with a deprecatory shrug. "The point is that if you died to-morrow where would be the security then?"

"I could insure my life, and make the policy over to you."

"Your premiums for such a sum, if any office would have you, which I very much doubt, would come to close on five hundred a year. That would hardly suit your book."

"Well, sir, what do you intend to propose?" asked the Admiral.

"I might, to accommodate you, work it in another way. I should send for a medical man, and have an opinion upon your life. Then I might see what could be done."

"That is quite fair. I have no objection to that."

"There is a very clever doctor in the street here. Proudie is his name. John, go and fetch Doctor Proudie." The youth was dispatched upon his errand, while Mr. Metaxa sat at his desk, trimming his nails, and shooting out little comments upon the weather. Presently feet were heard upon the stairs, the moneylender hurried out, there was a sound of whispering, and he returned with a large, fat, greasy-looking man, clad in a much worn frock-coat, and a very dilapidated top hat.

"Doctor Proudie, gentlemen," said Mr. Metaxa.

The doctor bowed, smiled, whipped off his hat, and produced his stethoscope from its interior with the air of a conjurer upon the stage. "Which of these gentlemen am I to examine?" he asked, blinking from one to the other of them. "Ah, it is you! Only your waistcoat! You need not undo your collar. Thank you! A full breath! Thank you! Ninety-nine! Thank you! Now hold your breath for a moment. Oh, dear, dear, what is this I hear?"

"What is it then?" asked the Admiral coolly.

"Tut! tut! This is a great pity. Have you had rheumatic fever?"

"Never."

"You have had some serious illness."

"Never."

"Ah, you are an admiral. You have been abroad, tropics, malaria, ague—I know."

"I have never had a day's illness."

"Not to your knowledge; but you have inhaled unhealthy air, and it has left its effect. You have an organic murmur—slight but distinct."

"Is it dangerous?"

"It might at any time become so. You should not take violent exercise."

"Oh, indeed. It would hurt me to run a half mile?"

"It would be very dangerous."

"And a mile?"

"Would be almost certainly fatal."

"Then there is nothing else the matter?"

"No. But if the heart is weak, then everything is weak, and the life is not a sound one."

"You see, Admiral," remarked Mr. Metaxa, as the doctor secreted his stethoscope once more in his hat, "my remarks were not entirely uncalled for. I am sorry that the doctor's opinion is not more favourable, but this is a matter of business, and certain obvious precautions must be taken."

"Of course. Then the matter is at an end."

"Well, we might even now do business. I am most anxious to be of use to you. How long do you think, doctor, that this gentleman will in all probability live?"

"Well, well, it's rather a delicate question to answer," said Mr. Proudie, with a show of embarrassment.

"Not a bit, sir. Out with it! I have faced death too often to flinch from it now, though I saw it as near me as you are."

"Well, well, we must go by averages of course. Shall we say two years? I should think that you have a full two years before you. In two years your pension would bring in £1,600. Now I will do my very best for you, Admiral! I will advance you £2,000, and you can make over to me your pension for your life. It is pure speculation on my part. If you die to-morrow I lose my money. If the doctor's prophecy is correct I shall still be out of pocket. If you live a little longer, then I may see my money again. It is the very best I can do for you."

"Then you wish to buy my pension?"

"Yes, for two thousand down."

"And if I live for twenty years?"

"Oh, in that case of course my speculation would be more successful. But you have heard the doctor's opinion."

"Would you advance the money instantly?"

"You should have a thousand at once. The other thousand I should expect you to take in furniture."

"In furniture?"

"Yes, Admiral. We shall do you a beautiful houseful at that sum. It is the custom of my clients to take half in furniture."

The Admiral sat in dire perplexity. He had come out to get money, and to go back without any, to be powerless to help when his boy needed every shilling to save him from disaster, that would be very bitter to him. On the other hand, it was so much that he surrendered, and so little that he received. Little, and yet something. Would it not be better than going back empty-handed? He saw the yellow backed cheque-book upon the table. The moneylender opened it and dipped his pen into the ink.

"Shall I fill it up?" said he.

"I think, Admiral," remarked Westmacott, "that we had better have a little walk and some luncheon before we settle this matter."

"Oh, we may as well do it at once. It would be absurd to postpone it now." Metaxa spoke with some heat, and his eyes glinted angrily from between his narrow lids at the imperturbable Charles. The Admiral was simple in money matters, but he had seen much of men and had learned to read them. He saw that venomous glance, and saw too that intense eagerness was peeping out from beneath the careless air which the agent had assumed.

"You're quite right, Westmacott," said he. "We'll have a little walk before we settle it."

"But I may not be here this afternoon."

"Then we must choose another day."

"But why not settle it now?"

"Because I prefer not," said the Admiral shortly.

"Very well. But remember that my offer is only for to-day. It is off unless you take it at once."

"Let it be off, then."

"There's my fee," cried the doctor.

"How much?"

"A guinea."

The Admiral threw a pound and a shilling upon the table. "Come, Westmacott," said he, and they walked together from the room.

"I don't like it," said Charles, when they found themselves in the street once more; "I don't profess to be a very sharp chap, but this is a trifle too thin. What did he want to go out and speak to the doctor for? And how very convenient this tale of a weak heart was! I believe they are a couple of rogues, and in league with each other."

"A shark and a pilot fish," said the Admiral.

"I'll tell you what I propose, sir. There's a lawyer named McAdam who does my aunt's business. He is a very honest fellow, and lives at the other side of Poultry. We'll go over to him together and have his opinion about the whole matter."

"How far is it to his place?"

"Oh, a mile at least. We can have a cab."

"A mile? Then we shall see if there is any truth in what that swab of a doctor said. Come, my boy, and clap on all sail, and see who can stay the longest."

Then the sober denizens of the heart of business London saw a singular sight as they returned from their luncheons. Down the roadway, dodging among cabs and carts, ran a weather-stained elderly man, with wide flapping black hat, and homely suit of tweeds. With elbows braced back, hands clenched near his armpits, and chest protruded, he scudded along, while close at his heels lumbered a large-limbed, heavy, yellow moustached young man, who seemed to feel the exercise a good deal more than his senior. On they dashed, helter-skelter, until they pulled up panting at the office where the lawyer of the Westmacotts was to be found.

"There now!" cried the Admiral in triumph. "What d'ye think of that? Nothing wrong in the engine-room, eh?"

"You seem fit enough, sir."

"Blessed if I believe the swab was a certificated doctor at all. He was flying false colours, or I am mistaken."

"They keep the directories and registers in this eating-house," said Westmacott. "We'll go and look him out."

They did so, but the medical rolls contained no such name as that of Dr. Proudie, of Bread Street.

"Pretty villainy this!" cried the Admiral, thumping his chest. "A dummy doctor and a vamped up disease. Well, we've tried the rogues, Westmacott! Let us see what we can do with your honest man."

The Admiral sprang back and raised his stick once more.

14
Eastward Ho!

Mr. McAdam, of the firm of McAdam and Squire, was a highly polished man who dwelt behind a highly polished table in the neatest and snuggest of offices. He was white-haired and amiable, with a deep-lined aquiline face, was addicted to low bows, and indeed, always seemed to carry himself at half-cock, as though just descending into one, or just recovering himself. He wore a high-buckled stock, took snuff, and adorned his conversation with little scraps from the classics.

"My dear sir," said he, when he had listened to their story, "any friend of Mrs. Westmacott's is a friend of mine. Try a pinch. I wonder that you should have gone to this man Metaxa. His advertisement is enough to condemn him. *Habet foenum in cornu.* They are all rogues."

"The doctor was a rogue too. I didn't like the look of him at the time."

"*Arcades ambo.* But now we must see what we can do for you. Of course what Metaxa said was perfectly right. The pension is in itself no security at all, unless it were accompanied by a life assurance which would be an income in itself. It is no good whatever."

His clients' faces fell.

"But there is the second alternative. You might sell the pension right out. Speculative investors occasionally deal in such things. I have one client, a sporting man, who would be very likely to take it up if we could agree upon terms. Of course, I must follow Metaxa's example by sending for the doctor."

For the second time was the Admiral punched and tapped and listened to. This time, however, there could be no question of the qualifications of the doctor, a well-known Fellow of the College of Surgeons, and his report was as favourable as the other's had been adverse.

"He has the heart and chest of a man of forty," said he. "I can recommend his life as one of the best of his age that I have ever examined."

"That's well," said Mr. McAdam, making a note of the doctor's remarks, while the Admiral disbursed a second guinea. "Your price, I understand, is five thousand pounds. I can communicate with Mr. Elberry, my client, and let you know whether he cares to touch the matter. Meanwhile you can leave your pension papers here, and I will give you a receipt for them."

"Very well. I should like the money soon."

"That is why I am retaining the papers. If I can see Mr. Elberry to-day we may let you have a cheque to-morrow. Try another pinch. No? Well, good-bye. I am happy to have been of service." Mr. McAdam bowed them out, for he was a very busy man, and they found themselves in the street once more with lighter hearts than when they had left it.

"Well, Westmacott, I am sure I am very much obliged to you," said the Admiral. "You have stood by me when I was the better for a little help, for I'm clean out of my soundings among these city sharks. But I've something to do now which is more in my own line, and I need not trouble you any more."

"Oh, it is no trouble. I have nothing to do. I never have anything to do. I don't suppose I could do it if I had. I should be delighted to come with you, sir, if I can be of any use."

"No, no, my lad. You go home again. It would be kind of you, though, if you would look in at number one when you get back and tell my wife that all's well with me, and that I'll be back in an hour or so."

"All right, sir. I'll tell her." Westmacott raised his hat and strode away to the westward, while the Admiral, after a hurried lunch, bent his steps towards the east.

It was a long walk, but the old seaman swung along at a rousing pace, leaving street after street behind him. The great business places dwindled down into commonplace shops and dwellings, which decreased and became more stunted, even as the folk who filled them did, until he was deep in the evil places of the eastern end. It was a land of huge, dark houses and of garish gin-shops, a land, too, where life moves irregularly and where adventures are to be gained—as the Admiral was to learn to his cost.

He was hurrying down one of the long, narrow, stone-flagged lanes between the double lines of crouching, dishevelled women and of dirty children who sat on the hollowed steps of the houses, and basked in the autumn sun. At one side was a barrowman with a load of walnuts, and beside the barrow a bedraggled woman with a black fringe and a chequered shawl thrown over her head. She was cracking walnuts and picking them out of the shells, throwing out a remark occasionally to a rough man in a rabbit-skin cap, with straps under the knees of his corduroy trousers, who stood puffing a black clay pipe with his back against the wall. What the cause of the quarrel was, or what sharp sarcasm from the woman's lips pricked suddenly through that thick skin may never be known, but suddenly the man took his pipe in his left hand, leaned forward, and deliberately struck her across the face with his right. It was a slap rather than a blow, but the woman gave a sharp cry and cowered up against the barrow with her hand to her cheek.

"You infernal villain!" cried the Admiral, raising his stick. "You brute and blackguard!"

"Garn!" growled the rough, with the deep rasping intonation of a savage. "Garn out o' this or I'll——" He took a step forward with uplifted hand, but in an instant down came cut number three upon his wrist, and cut number five across his thigh, and cut number one full in the center of his rabbit-skin cap. It was not a heavy stick, but it was strong enough to leave a good red weal wherever it fell. The rough yelled with pain, and rushed in, hitting with both hands, and kicking with his iron-shod boots, but the Admiral had still a quick foot and a true eye, so that he bounded backwards and sideways, still raining a shower of blows upon his savage antagonist. Suddenly, however, a pair of arms closed round his neck, and glancing backwards he caught a glimpse of the black coarse fringe of the woman whom he had befriended. "I've got him!" she shrieked. "I'll 'old 'im. Now, Bill, knock the tripe out of him!" Her grip was as strong as a man's, and her wrist pressed like an iron bar upon the Admiral's throat. He made a desperate effort to disengage himself, but the most that he could do was to swing her round, so as to place her between his adversary and himself. As it proved, it was the very best thing that he could have done. The rough, half-blinded and maddened by the blows which he had received, struck out with all his ungainly strength, just as his partner's head swung round in front of him. There was a noise like that of a stone hitting a wall, a deep groan, her grasp relaxed, and she dropped a dead weight upon the pavement, while the Admiral sprang back and raised his stick once more, ready either for attack or defense. Neither were needed, however, for at that moment there was a scattering of the crowd, and two police constables, burly and helmeted, pushed their way through the rabble. At the sight of them the rough took to his heels, and was instantly screened from view by a veil of his friends and neighbours.

"I have been assaulted," panted the Admiral. "This woman was attacked and I had to defend her."

"This is Bermondsey Sal," said one police officer, bending over the bedraggled heap of tattered shawl and dirty skirt. "She's got it hot this time."

"He was a shortish man, thick, with a beard."

"Ah, that's Black Davie. He's been up four times for beating her. He's about done the job now. If I were you I would let that sort settle their own little affairs, sir."

"Do you think that a man who holds the Queen's commission will stand by and see a woman struck?" cried the Admiral indignantly.

"Well, just as you like, sir. But you've lost your watch, I see."

"My watch!" He clapped his hand to his waistcoat. The chain was hanging down in front, and the watch gone.

He passed his hand over his forehead. "I would not have lost that watch for anything," said he. "No money could replace it. It was given my by the ship's company after our African cruise. It has an inscription."

The policeman shrugged his shoulders. "It comes from meddling," said he.

"What'll you give me if I tell yer where it is?" said a sharp-faced boy among the crowd. "Will you gimme a quid?"

"Certainly."

"Well, where's the quid?"

The Admiral took a sovereign from his pocket. "Here it is."

"Then 'ere's the ticker!" The boy pointed to the clenched hand of the senseless woman. A glimmer of gold shone out from between the fingers, and on opening them up, there was the Admiral's chronometer. This interesting victim had throttled her protector with one hand, while she had robbed him with the other.

The Admiral left his address with the policeman, satisfied that the woman was only stunned, not dead, and then set off upon his way once more, the poorer perhaps in his faith in human nature, but in very good spirits none the less. He walked with dilated nostrils and clenched hands, all glowing and tingling with the excitement of the combat, and warmed with the thought that he could still, when there was need, take his own part in a street brawl in spite of his three-score and odd years.

His way now led towards the river-side regions, and a cleansing whiff of tar was to be detected in the stagnant autumn air. Men with the blue jersey and peaked cap of the boatman, or the white ducks of the dockers, began to replace the corduroys and fustian of the labourers. Shops with nautical instruments in the windows, rope and paint sellers, and slop shops with long rows of oilskins dangling from hooks, all proclaimed the neighbourhood of the docks. The Admiral quickened his pace and straightened his figure as his surroundings became more nautical, until at last, peeping between two high, dingy wharfs, he caught a glimpse of the mud-coloured waters of the Thames, and of the bristle of masts and funnels which rose from its broad bosom. To the right lay a quiet street, with many brass plates upon either side, and wire blinds in all of the windows. The Admiral walked slowly down it until "The Saint Lawrence Shipping Company" caught his eye. He crossed the road, pushed open the door, and found himself in a low-ceilinged office, with a long counter at one end and a great number of wooden sections of ships stuck upon boards and plastered all over the walls.

"Is Mr. Henry in?" asked the Admiral.

"No, sir," answered an elderly man from a high seat in the corner. "He has not come to town to-day. I can manage any business you may wish seen to."

"You don't happen to have a first or second officer's place vacant, do you?"

The manager looked with a dubious eye at his singular applicant.

"Do you hold certificates?" he asked.

"I hold every nautical certificate there is."

"Then you won't do for us."

"Why not?"

"Your age, sir."

"I give you my word that I can see as well as ever, and am as good a man in every way."

"I don't doubt it."

"Why should my age be a bar, then?"

"Well, I must put it plainly. If a man of your age, holding certificates, has not got past a second officer's berth, there must be a black mark against him somewhere. I won't know what it is, drink or temper, or want of judgment, but something there must be."

"I assure you there is nothing, but I find myself stranded, and so have to turn to the old business again."

"Oh, that's it," said the manager, with suspicion in his eye. "How long were you in your last billet?"

"Fifty-one years."

"What!"

"Yes, sir, one-and-fifty years."

"In the same employ?"

"Yes."

"Why, you must have begun as a child."

"I was twelve when I joined."

"It must be a strangely managed business," said the manager, "which allows men to leave it who have served for fifty years, and who are still as good as ever. Who did you serve?"

"The Queen. Heaven bless her!"

"Oh, you were in the Royal Navy. What rating did you hold?"

"I am Admiral of the Fleet."

The manager started, and sprang down from his high stool.

"My name is Admiral Hay Denver. There is my card. And here are the records of my service. I don't, you understand, want to push another man from his billet; but if you should chance to have a berth open, I should be very glad of it. I know the navigation from the Cod Banks right up to Montreal a great deal better than I know the streets of London."

The astonished manager glanced over the blue papers which his visitor had handed him. "Won't you take a chair, Admiral?" said he.

"Thank you! But I should be obliged if you would drop my title now. I told you because you asked me, but I've left the quarter-deck, and I am plain Mr. Hay Denver now."

"May I ask," said the manager, "are you the same Denver who commanded at one time on the North American station?"

"I did."

"Then it was you who got one of our boats, the *Comus,* off the rocks in the Bay of Fundy? The directors voted you three hundred guineas as salvage, and you refused them."

"It was an offer which should not have been made," said the Admiral sternly.

"Well, it reflects credit upon you that you should think so. If Mr. Henry were here I am sure that he would arrange this matter for you at once. As it is, I shall lay it before the directors to-day, and I am sure that they will be proud to have you in our employment, and, I hope, in some more suitable position than that which you suggest."

"I am very much obliged to you, sir," said the Admiral, and started off again, well pleased, upon his homeward journey.

Clara and the Doctor were sitting together in the dining-room.

15
Still Among Shoals

NEXT DAY brought the Admiral a cheque for £5,000 from Mr. McAdam, and a stamped agreement by which he made over his pension papers to the speculative investor. It was not until he had signed and sent it off that the full significance of all that he had done broke upon him. He had sacrificed everything. His pension was gone. He had nothing save only what he could earn. But the stout old heart never quailed. He waited eagerly for a letter from the Saint Lawrence Shipping Company, and in the meanwhile he gave his landlord a quarter's notice. Hundred pound a year houses would in future be a luxury which he could not aspire to. A small lodging in some inexpensive part of London must be the substitute for his breezy Norwood villa. So be it, then! Better that a thousand fold than that his name should be associated with failure and disgrace.

On the morning Harold Denver was to meet the creditors of the firm, and to explain the situation to them. It was a hateful task, a degrading task, but he set himself to do it with quiet resolution. At home they waited in intense anxiety to learn the result of the meeting. It was late before he returned, haggard and pale, like a man who has done and suffered much.

"What's this board in front of the house?" he asked.

"We are going to try a little change of scene," said the Admiral. "This place is neither town nor country. But never mind that, boy. Tell us what happened in the City."

"God help me! My wretched business is driving you out of house and home!" cried Harold, broken down by this fresh evidence of the effects of his misfortunes. "It is easier for me to meet my creditors than to see you two suffering so patiently for my sake."

"Tut, tut!" cried the Admiral. "There's no suffering in the matter. Mother would rather be near the theatres. That's at the bottom of it, isn't it, mother? You come and sit down here between us and tell us all about it."

Harold sat down with a loving hand in each of his.

"It's not so bad as we thought," said he, "and yet it is bad enough. I have about ten days to find the money, but I don't know which way to turn for it. Pearson, however, lied, as usual, when he spoke of £13,000. The amount is not quite £7,000."

The Admiral clapped his hands. "I knew we should weather it after all! Hurrah, my boy! Hip, hip, hip, hurrah!"

Harold gazed at him in surprise, while the old seaman waved his arm above his head and bellowed out three stentorian cheers. "Where am I to get seven thousand pounds from, dad?" he asked.

"Never mind. You spin your yarn."

"Well, they were very good and very kind, but of course they must have either their money or their money's worth. They passed a vote of sympathy with me, and agreed to wait ten days before they took any proceedings. Three of them, whose claim came to £3,500, told me that if I would give them my personal I.O.U., and pay interest at the rate of five per cent., their amounts might stand over as long as I wished. That would be a charge of £175 upon my income, but with economy I could meet it, and it diminishes the debt by one-half."

Again the Admiral burst out cheering.

"There remains, therefore, about £3,200, which has to be found within ten days. No man shall lose by me. I gave them my word in the room that if I worked my soul out of my body every one of them should be paid. I shall not spend a penny upon myself until it is done. But some of them can't wait. They are poor men themselves, and must have their money. They have issued a warrant for Pearson's arrest. But they think that he has got away to the States."

"These men *shall* have their money," said the Admiral.

"Dad!"

"Yes, my boy, you don't know the resources of the family. One never does know until one tries. What have you yourself now?"

"I have about a thousand pounds invested."

"All right. And I have about as much more. There's a good start. Now, mother, it is your turn. What is that little bit of paper of yours?"

Mrs. Denver unfolded it, and placed it upon Harold's knee.

"Five thousand pounds!" he gasped.

"Ah, but mother is not the only rich one. Look at this!" And the Admiral unfolded his cheque, and placed it upon the other knee.

Harold gazed from one to the other in bewilderment. "Ten thousand pounds!" he cried. "Good heavens! where did these come from?"

"You will not worry any longer, dear," murmured his mother, slipping her arm round him.

But his quick eye had caught the signature upon one of the cheques. "Doctor Walker!" he cried, flushing. "This is Clara's doing. Oh, dad, we cannot take this money. It would not be right nor honourable."

"No, boy, I am glad you think so. It is something, however, to have proved one's friend, for a real good friend he is. It was he who brought it in, though Clara sent him. But this other money will be enough to cover everything, and it is all my own."

"Your own? Where did you get it, dad?"

"Tut, tut! See what it is to have a City man to deal with. It is my own, and fairly earned, and that is enough."

"Dear old dad!" Harold squeezed his gnarled hand. "And you, mother! You have lifted the trouble from my heart. I feel another man. You have saved my honour, my good name, everything. I cannot owe you more, for I owe you everything already."

So while the autumn sunset shone ruddily through the broad window these three sat together hand in hand, with hearts which were too full to speak. Suddenly the soft thudding of tennis balls was heard, and Mrs. Westmacott bounded into view upon the lawn with brandished racket and short skirts fluttering in the breeze. The sight came as a relief to their strained nerves, and they burst all three into a hearty fit of laughter.

"She is playing with her nephew," said Harold at last. "The Walkers have not come out yet. I think that it would be well if you were to give me that cheque, mother, and I were to return it in person."

"Certainly, Harold. I think it would be very nice."

He went in through the garden. Clara and the Doctor were sitting together in the dining-room. She sprang to her feet at the sight of him.

"Oh, Harold, I have been waiting for you so impatiently," she cried; "I saw you pass the front windows half an hour ago. I would have come in if I dared. Do tell us what has happened."

"I have come in to thank you both. How can I repay you for your kindness? Here is your cheque, Doctor. I have not needed it. I find that I can lay my hands on enough to pay my creditors."

"Thank God!" said Clara fervently.

"The sum is less than I thought, and our resources considerably more. We have been able to do it with ease."

"With ease!" The Doctor's brow clouded and his manner grew cold. "I think, Harold, that you would do better to take this money of mine, than to use that which seems to you to be gained with ease."

"Thank you, sir. If I borrowed from any one it would be from you. But my father has this very sum, five thousand pounds, and, as I tell him, I owe him so much that I have no compunction about owing him more."

"No compunction! Surely there are some sacrifices which a son should not allow his parents to make."

"Sacrifices! What do you mean?"

"Is it possible that you do not know how this money has been obtained?"

"I give you my word, Doctor Walker, that I have no idea. I asked my father, but he refused to tell me."

"I thought not," said the Doctor, the gloom clearing from his brow. "I was sure that you were not a man who, to clear yourself from a little money difficulty, would sacrifice the happiness of your mother and the health of your father."

"Good gracious! what do you mean?"

"It is only right that you should know. That money represents the commutation of your father's pension. He has reduced himself to poverty, and intends to go to sea again to earn a living."

"To sea again! Impossible!"

"It is the truth! Charles Westmacott has told Ida. He was with him in the City when he took his poor pension about from dealer to dealer trying to sell it. He succeeded at last, and hence the money."

"He has sold his pension!" cried Harold, with his hands to his face. "My dear old dad has sold his pension!" He rushed from the room, and burst wildly into the presence of his parents once more. "I cannot take it, father," he cried. "Better bankruptcy than that. Oh, if I had only known your plan! We must have back the pension. Oh, mother, mother, how could you think me capable of such selfishness? Give me the cheque, dad, and I will see this man to-night, for I would sooner die like a dog in the ditch than touch a penny of this money."

16
A Midnight Visitor

Now all this time, while the tragi-comedy of life was being played in these three suburban villas, while on a commonplace stage love and humour and fears and lights and shadows were so swiftly succeeding each other, and while these three families, drifted together by fate, were shaping each other's destinies and working out in their own fashion the strange, intricate ends of human life, there were human eyes which watched over every stage of the performance, and which were keenly critical of every actor on it. Across the road beyond the green palings of the close-cropped lawn, behind the curtains of their creeper-framed windows, sat the two old ladies, Miss Bertha and Miss Monica Williams, looking out as from a private box at all that was being enacted before them. The growing friendship of the three families, the engagement of Harold Denver with Clara Walker, the engagement of Charles Westmacott with her sister, the dangerous fascination which the widow exercised over the Doctor, the preposterous behaviour of the Walker girls and the unhappiness which they had caused their father, not one of these incidents escaped the notice of the two maiden ladies. Bertha the younger had a smile or a sigh for the lovers, Monica the elder a frown or a shrug for the elders. Every night they talked over what they had seen, and their own dull, uneventful life took a warmth and a colouring from their neighbours as a blank wall reflects a beacon fire.

And now it was destined that they should experience the one keen sensation of their later years, the one memorable incident from which all future incidents should be dated.

It was on the very night which succeeded the events which have just been narrated, when suddenly into Monica Williams's head, as she tossed upon her sleepless bed, there shot a thought which made her sit up with a thrill and a gasp.

"Bertha," said she, plucking at the shoulder of her sister, "I have left the front window open."

"No, Monica, surely not." Bertha sat up also, and thrilled in sympathy.

"I am sure of it. You remember I had forgotten to water the pots, and then I opened the window, and Jane called me about the jam, and I have never been in the room since."

"Good gracious, Monica, it is a mercy that we have not been murdered in our beds. There was a house broken into at Forest Hill last week. Shall we go down and shut it?"

"I dare not go down alone, dear, but if you will come with me. Put on your slippers and dressing-gown. We do not need a candle. Now, Bertha, we will go down together."

Two little white patches moved vaguely through the darkness, the stairs creaked, the door whined, and they were at the front room window. Monica closed it gently down, and fastened the snib.

"What a beautiful moon!" said she, looking out. "We can see as clearly as if it were day. How peaceful and quiet the three houses are over yonder! It seems quite sad to see that 'To Let' card upon number one. I wonder how number two will like their going. For my part I could better spare that dreadful woman at number three with her short skirts and her snake. But, oh, Bertha, look! look!! look!!!" Her voice had fallen suddenly to a quivering whisper and she was pointing to the Westmacotts' house. Her sister gave a gasp of horror, and stood with a clutch at Monica's arm, staring in the same direction.

There was a light in the front room, a slight, wavering light such as would be given by a small candle or taper. The blind was down, but the light shone dimly through. Outside in the garden, with his figure outlined against the luminous square, there stood a man, his back to the road, his two hands upon the window ledge, and his body rather bent as though he were trying to peep in past the blind. So absolutely still and motionless was he that in spite of the moon they might well have overlooked him were it not for that telltale light behind.

"Good heaven!" gasped Bertha, "it is a burglar."

But her sister set her mouth grimly and shook her head. "We shall see," she whispered. "It may be something worse."

Swiftly and furtively the man stood suddenly erect, and began to push the window slowly up. Then he put one knee upon the sash, glanced round to see that all was safe, and climbed over into the room. As he did so he had to push the blind aside. Then the two spectators saw where the light came from. Mrs. Westmacott was standing, as rigid as a statue, in the centre of the room, with a lighted taper in her right hand. For an instant they caught a glimpse of her stern face and her white collar. Then the blind fell back into position, and the two figures disappeared from their view.

"Oh, that dreadful woman!" cried Monica. "That dreadful, dreadful woman! She was waiting for him. You saw it with your own eyes, sister Bertha!"

"Hush, dear, hush and listen!" said her more charitable companion. They pushed their own window up once more, and watched from behind the curtains.

For a long time all was silent within the house. The light still stood motionless as though Mrs. Westmacott remained rigidly in the one position, while from time to time a shadow passed in front of it to show that her midnight visitor was pacing up and down in front of her. Once they saw his outline clearly, with his hands outstretched as if in appeal or entreaty. Then suddenly there was a dull sound, a cry, the noise of a fall, the taper was extinguished, and a dark figure fled in the moonlight, rushed across the garden, and vanished amid the shrubs at the farther side.

Then only did the two old ladies understand that they had looked on whilst a tragedy had been enacted. "Help!" they cried, and "Help!" in their high, thin voices, timidly at first, but gathering volume as they went on, until The Wilderness rang with their shrieks. Lights shone in all the windows opposite, chains rattled, bars were unshot, doors opened, and out rushed friends to the rescue. Harold, with a stick; the Admiral, with his sword, his grey head and bare feet protruding from either end of a long brown ulster; finally, Doctor Walker, with a poker, all ran to the help of the Westmacotts. Their door had been already opened, and they crowded tumultuously into the front room.

Charles Westmacott, white to the lips, was kneeling on the floor, supporting his aunt's head upon his knee.

She lay outstretched, dressed in her ordinary clothes, the extinguished taper still grasped in her hand, no mark or wound upon her—pale, placid, and senseless.

"Thank God you are come, Doctor," said Charles, looking up. "Do tell me how she is, and what I should do."

Doctor Walker kneeled beside her, and passed his left hand over her head, while he grasped her pulse with the right.

"She has had a terrible blow," said he. "It must have been with some blunt weapon. Here is the place behind the ear. But she is a woman of extraordinary physical powers. Her pulse is full and slow. There is no stertor. It is my belief that she is merely stunned, and that she is in no danger at all."

"Thank God for that!"

"We must get her to bed. We shall carry her upstairs, and then I shall send my girls in to her. But who has done this?"

"Some robber," said Charles. "You see that the window is open. She must have heard him and come down, for she was always perfectly fearless. I wish to goodness she had called me."

"But she was dressed."

"Sometimes she sits up very late."

"I did sit up very late," said a voice. She had opened her eyes, and was blinking at them in the lamplight. "A villain came in through the window and struck me with a life-preserver. You can tell the police so when they come. Also that it was a little fat man. Now, Charles, give me your arm and I shall go upstairs."

But her spirit was greater than her strength, for as she staggered to her feet, her head swam round, and she would have fallen again had her nephew not thrown his arms round her. They carried her upstairs among them and laid her upon the bed, where the Doctor watched beside her, while Charles went off to the police-station, and the Denvers mounted guard over the frightened maids.

17
In Port at Last

DAY had broken before the several denizens of The Wilderness had all returned to their homes, the police finished their inquiries, and all come back to its normal quiet. Mrs. Westmacott had been left sleeping peacefully with a small chloral draught to steady her nerves and a handkerchief soaked in arnica bound round her head. It was with some surprise, therefore, that the Admiral received a note from her about ten o'clock, asking him to be good enough to step in to her. He hurried in, fearing that she might have taken some turn for the worse, but he was reassured to find her sitting up in her bed, with Clara and Ida Walker in attendance upon her. She had removed the handkerchief, and had put on a little cap with pink ribbons, and a maroon dressing-jacket, daintily fulled at the neck and sleeves.

"My dear friend," said she as he entered, "I wish to make a last few remarks to you. No, no," she continued, laughing, as she saw a look of dismay upon his face. "I shall not dream of dying for at least another thirty years. A woman should be ashamed to die before she is seventy. I wish, Clara, that you would ask your father to step up. And you, Ida, just pass me my cigarettes, and open me a bottle of stout."

"Now then," she continued, as the Doctor joined their party. "I don't quite know what I ought to say to you, Admiral. You want some very plain speaking to."

"'Pon my word, ma'am, I don't know what you are talking about."

"The idea of you at your age talking of going to sea, and leaving that dear, patient little wife of yours at home, who has seen nothing of you all her life! It's all very well for you. You have the life, and the change, and the excitement, but you don't think of her eating her heart out in a dreary London lodging. You men are all the same."

"Well, ma'am, since you know so much, you probably know also that I have sold my pension. How am I to live if I do not turn my hand to work?"

Mrs. Westmacott produced a large registered envelope from beneath the sheets and tossed it over to the old seaman.

"That excuse won't do. There are your pension papers. Just see if they are right."

He broke the seal, and out tumbled the very papers which he had made over to McAdam two days before.

"But what am I to do with these now?" he cried in bewilderment.

"You will put them in a safe place, or get a friend to do so, and, if you do your duty, you will go to your wife and beg her pardon for having even for an instant thought of leaving her."

The Admiral passed his hand over his rugged forehead. "This is very good of you, ma'am," said he, "very good and kind, and I know that you are a staunch friend, but for all that these papers mean money, and though we may have been in broken water lately, we are not quite in such straits as to have to signal to our friends. When we do, ma'am, there's no one we would look to sooner than to you."

"Don't be ridiculous!" said the widow. "You know

nothing whatever about it, and yet you stand there laying down the law. I'll have my way in the matter, and you shall take the papers, for it is no favour that I am doing you, but simply a restoration of stolen property."

"How that, ma'am?"

"I am just going to explain, though you might take a lady's word for it without asking any questions. Now, what I am going to say is just between you four, and must go no farther. I have my own reasons for wishing to keep it from the police. Who do you think it was who struck me last night, Admiral?"

"Some villain, ma'am. I don't know his name."

"But I do. It was the same man who ruined or tried to ruin your son. It was my only brother, Jeremiah."

"Ah!"

"I will tell you about him—or a little about him, for he has done much which I would not care to talk of, nor you to listen to. He was always a villain, smooth-spoken and plausible, but a dangerous, subtle villain all the same. If I have some hard thoughts about mankind I can trace them back to the childhood which I spent with my brother. He is my only living relative, for my other brother, Charles's father, was killed in the Indian mutiny.

"Our father was rich, and when he died he made a good provision both for Jeremiah and for me. He knew Jeremiah and he mistrusted him, however; so instead of giving him all that he meant him to have he handed me over a part of it, telling me, with what was almost his dying breath, to hold it in trust for my brother, and to use it in his behalf when he should have squandered or lost all that he had. This arrangement was meant to be a secret between my father and myself, but unfortunately his words were overheard by the nurse, and she repeated them afterwards to my brother, so that he came to know that I held some money in trust for him. I suppose tobacco will not harm my head, Doctor? Thank you, then I shall trouble you for the matches, Ida." She lit a cigarette, and leaned back upon the pillow, with the blue wreaths curling from her lips.

"I cannot tell you how often he has attempted to get that money from me. He has bullied, cajoled, threatened, coaxed, done all that a man could do. I still held it with the presentiment that a need for it would come. When I heard of this villainous business, his flight, and his leaving his partner to face the storm, above all that my old friend had been driven to surrender his income in order to make up for my brother's defalcations, I felt that now indeed I had a need for it. I sent in Charles yesterday to Mr. McAdam, and his client, upon hearing the facts of the case, very graciously consented to give back the papers, and to take the money which he had advanced. Not a word of thanks to me, Admiral. I tell you that it was very cheap benevolence, for it was all done with his own money, and how could I use it better?

"I thought that I should probably hear from him soon, and I did. Last evening there was handed in a note of the usual whining, cringing tone. He had come back from abroad at the risk of his life and liberty, just in order that he might say good-bye to the only sister he ever had, and to entreat my forgiveness for any pain which he had caused me. He would never trouble me again, and he begged only that I would hand over to him the sum which I held in trust for him. That, with what he had already, would be enough to start him as an honest man in the new world, when he would ever remember and pray for the dear sister who had been his saviour. That was the style of the letter, and it ended by imploring me to leave the window-latch open, and to be in the front room at three in the morning, when he would come to receive my last kiss and to bid me farewell.

"Bad as he was, I could not, when he trusted me, betray him. I said nothing, but I was there at the hour. He entered through the window, and implored me to give him the money. He was terribly changed; gaunt, wolfish, and spoke like a madman. I told him that I had spent the money. He gnashed his teeth at me, and swore it was his money. I told him that I had spent it on him. He asked me how. I said in trying in make him an honest man, and in repairing the results of his villainy. He shrieked out a curse, and pulling something out of the breast of his coat—a loaded stick, I think—he struck me with it, and I remembered nothing more."

"The blackguard!" cried the Doctor, "but the police must be hot upon his track."

"I fancy not," Mrs. Westmacott answered calmly. "As my brother is a particularly tall, thin man, and as the police are looking for a short, fat one, I do not think that it is very probable that they will catch him. It is best, I think, that these little family matters should be adjusted in private."

"My dear ma'am," said the Admiral, "if it is indeed this man's money that has bought back my pension, then I can have no scruples about taking it. You have brought sunshine upon us, ma'am, when the clouds were at their darkest, for here is my boy who insists upon returning the money which I got. He can keep it now to pay his debts. For what you have done I can only ask God to bless you, ma'am, and as to thanking you I can't even ——"

"Then pray don't try," said the widow. "Now run away, Admiral, and make your peace with Mrs. Denver. I am sure if I were she it would be a long time before I should forgive you. As for me, I am going to America when Charles goes. You'll take me so far, won't you, Ida? There is a college being built in Denver which is to equip the woman of the future for the struggle of life, and especially for her battle against man. Some months ago the committee offered me a responsible situation upon the staff, and I have decided now to accept it, for Charles's marriage removes the last tie which binds me to England. You will write to me sometimes, my friends, you will address your letters to Professor Westmacott, Emancipation College, Denver. From there I shall watch how the glorious struggle goes in conservative old England, and if I am needed you will find me here again fighting in the forefront of the fray. Good-bye—but not you, girls; I have still a word I wish to say to you.

"Give me your hand, Ida, and yours, Clara," said she when they were alone. "Oh, you naughty little pusses, aren't you ashamed to look me in the face? Did you think—did you really think that I was so very blind, and could not see your little plot? You did it very well, I must say that, and really I think that I like you better as you are. But you had all your pains for nothing, you little conspirators, for I give you my word that I had quite made up my mind not to have him."

And so within a few weeks our little ladies from their observatory saw a mighty bustle in The Wilderness, when two-horse carriages came, and coachmen with favours, to bear away the twos who were destined to come back one. And they themselves in their crackling silk dresses went across, as invited, to the big double wedding breakfast which was held in the house of Doctor Walker. Then there was health-drinking, and laughter, and changing of dresses, and rice-throwing when the carriages drove up again, and two more couples started on that journey which ends only with life itself.

Charles Westmacott is now a flourishing ranchman in the western part of Texas, where he and his sweet little wife are the two most popular persons in all that county. Of their aunt they see little, but from time to time they see notices in the papers that there is a focus of light in Denver, where mighty thunderbolts are being forged which will one day bring the dominant sex upon their knees. The Admiral and his wife still live at number one, while Harold and Clara have taken number two, where Doctor Walker continues to reside. As to the business, it had been reconstructed, and the energy and ability of the junior partner had soon made up for all the ill that had been done by his senior. Yet with his sweet and refined home atmosphere he is able to realize his wish, and to keep himself free from the sordid aims and base ambitions which drag down the man whose business lies too exclusively in the money market of the vast Babylon. As he goes back every evening from the crowds of Throgmorton Street to the tree-lined peaceful avenues of Norwood, so he has found it possible in spirit also to do one's duties amidst the babel of the City, and yet to live beyond it.

Afterword

"If we could fly out of that window hand in hand," Sherlock Holmes tells Dr. Watson in a distinctly Peter Pan mood, "hover over this great city, gently remove the roofs, and peep in at the queer things which are going on, the strange coincidences, the plannings, the cross-purposes, the wonderful chains of events, working through generations, and leading to the most *outré* results, it would make all fiction with its conventionalities and foreseen conclusions most stale and unprofitable."

The vision of the Baker Street duo, hands joined, poised above the chimneys of London like airy spirits or tremulous fairies, is surely one of that Saga's most delicious moments. Not long before A. Conan Doyle penned that wonderful passage, he completed work on a novel whose aim was to enable readers to hover, peep in, and observe life in just such a manner. The setting was removed from the great metropolis, the story city of Holmes and his attentive chronicler, and transferred to the quiet, tree-lined suburb of Norwood. There, we find Doyle's characters living far from the reek, the rush, the madding crowd, and the jostling cabs of London. But not too far. The city can be heard and seen from that distance. It has long since sent out its advanced scouts and planted its outposts of progress:

From afar, when the breeze came from the north, the dull, low roar of the great city might be heard, like the breaking of the tide of life, while along the horizon might be seen the dim curtain of smoke, the grim spray which that tide threw up. Gradually, however, as the years passed, the City had thrown out a long brick-feeler here and there, curving, extending, coalescing, until at last the little cottages had been gripped round by these red tentacles, and had been absorbed to make room for the modern villa. Field by field, the estate. . .had been sold to the speculative builder, and had borne rich crops of snug suburban dwellings, arranged in curving crescents and tree-lined avenues.

A way of life is ending and a new way of living is beginning. The pleasures of an older, more spacious, pastoral England have yielded to the roads and rentals of the suburban developer. From empty fields rise sixteen-room, Swiss-built villas—"no basement, electric bells, hot and cold water, and every modern convenience, including a common tennis lawn." The telephone, the automobile, motion pictures, and flying machines are just around the corner. These are the last years of the old century and the old Queen.

Beyond the City gently removes the roofs of several such villas, and makes us intimate witnesses to the history of three families, "drifted together by fate, [who] were shaping each other's destinies and working out in their own fashion the strange, intricate ends of human life." What Sherlock Holmes once conjectured in a mood of playful fantasy is here made fact. With clinical skill, Dr. Doyle places the strange new species, *civis suburbanus Britannicae,* under the microscope. The storytelling warmth and wit of the scientist soon transform his exotic specimens into recognizable human beings who care for one another and about whom we, in turn, care. In that sense, this is an old-fashioned novel. In its close psychological and sociological focus, however, the novel is a good example of the modern. The reader has the best of both worlds.

Beyond the City was the author's summer writing project for the year 1891. It was a memorable year, a milestone year, for Conan Doyle. Something unexpected, something tremendous, happened to him even before the novel was published. The July and August appearances of "A Scandal in Bohemia" and "The Red-Headed League" in the *Strand* magazine made the novelist an overnight sensation—as a short story writer.

On June 1 of that *annus mirabilis,* Doyle noted in his diary that he had made an agreement with the magazine *Good Words* to write a 42,000-word novel for delivery by the first day of September. Though he kept the requisite cheerful mood more or less intact throughout the writing, Doyle preferred not to make the novel a full summer's labour. He reserved the last two weeks in August to go abroad and play cricket for the English team against United Holland, and he may have sensed that he would need to make more time available for plotting and writing Sherlock Holmes short stories for the *Strand.* At any rate, working quickly and steadily, and modelling his book in part on the observable life around him in his own suburban *milieu,* the novelist went forward with the same brisk pace at which his Norwood neighbours saw him pedal his bicycle during writing breaks, and the observant reader may note how the rush of hurried composition occasionally ruffles the placid surface of an otherwise impeccably serene narrative. It is a good guess, however, whether such bursts of headlong celerity may not be Doyle's characteristic way of rousing reticent characters to action and purpose. The novel certainly shows him to be the master of his storytelling tools, though it may be fairly objected that, at the end, the master is rather too eager to lay his tools back in the box. One suspects he was in a hurry to get out his cricket kit and get on with Holmes.

Whether Doyle's neighbours recognized themselves in the book, I have no way of knowing; but the bicycle, the energy, the optimism, the pawky humour, and the earnestness of Doyle himself are clearly on display. So, too, is a side of Doyle that is today very little understood or appreciated, and that is his attitude toward female emancipation. Influenced by his strong-willed mother, who drilled tiny Arthur on the fine points of courtesy, compassion, and *noblesse oblige,* and by Dr. Joseph Bell, his Edinburgh medical mentor, who advocated the admission of all qualified women to the medical school, it is not surprising that Doyle shows us a generous recognition of the rights of women. It will only come as a surprise to those who primarily remember Doyle's doubts about votes for women (too divisive for the peace of the home) and his criticism of the violent tactics of more militant Suffragettes (too uncivilized to do their movement any good). The portrait of the writer as a conservative chauvinist may be a widely accepted one, but it is a misleading depiction, one which does scant justice to his actual attitudes.

In fact, Conan Doyle was anything but a foe of feminism. Many of his positions on women's issues were surprisingly progressive. He worked for the reform of laws which discriminated against women, took a leaf from Bell's notebook and advocated the free entry of women into universities and professions, and supported votes for women after the war work of nurses and other volunteers had changed his mind on this issue. "He had an open mind," Dame Jean Conan Doyle has recently recollected of her father, "and admitted past misjudgements, so perhaps he had accepted the justice of their cause by then. . . . He certainly didn't underestimate women's intelligence; he encouraged his young Mary to become a journalist and often discussed possible careers for me."

With this in mind, let us return now to the Norwood of 1891. Doyle himself had moved there—to No. 12 Tennison Road—on June 25, after several weeks of scouting the area for a new home. He had given up his incredibly unprofitable ophthalmological practice in London. Not a single patient—not one!—had ever crossed the theshold of his consulting-room at 2 Devonshire Place, where the good doctor sat writing the first few Sherlock Holmes stories to pass the time of day and to earn back the fees that London's nearsighted and farsighted citizens never brought in.

Removed from London, Doyle embraced his increasingly profitable writing profession as a full-time activity. The large, red-bricked country home on Tennison Road ("A suitable house," Doyle recalled, "modest but comfortable, isolated and yet one of a row") was as much a confirmation of his new-found success as the mythical rooms on Baker Street. It was there, beyond the city, that Doyle completed the bulk of the *Adventures* of Sherlock Holmes and all of the *Memoirs,* stories which created a new urban myth. Before this, in *Beyond the City,* he managed to create a new suburban myth, transmuting his country neighbours and surroundings into fiction. Weeks of patient house-hunting, interviews, and bicycle sightseeing lent themselves easily and fluently to storytelling; the novel must already have been well advanced by the time he finally unpacked the last of the colourful sports equipment which makes its untidy appearance in the first chapter.

Work on *Beyond the City* went even more rapidly than Doyle himself might have expected. He finished his writing a little more than a month after his initial diary entry recorded his agreement to write. The novel went off on July 8, only two weeks after Doyle had settled in with wife Louise and two-year-old daughter Mary, and the writer was rewarded with a fee of £150—six times what he realized on the outright sale, five years before, of his first book, *A Study in Scarlet.* Obviously, Doyle's stock as a novelist was rising. So, too, judging by this congenial novel, was his skill. Beyond the fresh, crisp, workmanlike performance which we might expect from so thorough a professional is the appeal of a new fictional idea and a new character type.

But it was Holmes of London, not the secrets of suburbanites, for which Doyle's readers clamoured. Norwood was neither city nor country, and though Holmes was later to investigate the mysterious disappearance of a Norwood builder named Jonas Oldacre, no legendary detective had his locus there. The furor over Sherlock Holmes all but eclipsed *Beyond the City* when it débuted in the 1891 Christmas number of the sedate old *Good Words,* and in its initial British book publication it was eclipsed a second time by being set in the penumbra of *The Great Shadow,* a Napoleonic novel with which it was incongruously paired. The result of the pairing was predictable: lovers of Doyle's history novels read *The Great Shadow* and ignored *Beyond the City*; lovers of Sherlock Holmes ignored both. At least one American publisher thought the Norwood novel good enough to stand separately, but this edition was hardly a compliment to its author, as Conan Doyle himself recalled, with a chuckle, in his memoirs:

> It was pirated in New York just before the new Copyright Act came into force [in 1893], and the rascal publisher, thinking that a portrait—any sort of portrait—of the author would look well upon the cover, and being quite ignorant of my identity, put a very pretty and over-dressed young woman as my presentment. I still preserve a copy of this most flattering representation.

In the shadow of Sherlock Holmes, the Napoleon of Crime, and Napoleon himself, it is no wonder that *Beyond the City* suffered neglect. With the rattle of the London detective's hansom cabs and flying expresses, and with the massed charges of the French Emperor's trumpeting cavalry, ringing in their ears, readers had every right to be distracted.

A novel of quiet charm and mild melodrama, *Beyond the City* simply could not compete with the popular epics of Doyle's pen. It was unable to take advantage of those elements of high heroic action and adventure which Doyle had already made his trademark in the commercially successful exploits of *Micah Clarke* and *The White Company*. It could not showcase those elements of mystery and suspense in whose manipulation Doyle proved himself an adroit master, not only in the first two series of Sherlock Holmes stories but in the subsequent *Round the Fire* thrillers which revived hope (justifiably, as it turned out) for the imminent return of the great sleuth. Finally, the traditionally masculine hero was shunted aside by a two-fisted heroine who smoked, drank, debated, and demanded her complete liberty and equality. No wonder Victorian and later readers had second thoughts about this offbeat suburban chronicle! It seemed atypical and eccentric, unworthy of Doyle.

And yet *Beyond the City* is a novel well worth any reader's attention. The merits of the book may be uneven, but they are real merits, and it is my belief that they far outweigh the defects. I think it a reading experience that any Doyle fan ought not to miss, especially if he wishes to enhance his education about Doyle the writer and man. On some points, the novel does not even compare unfavourably with Doyle's best work. Many people read the Sherlock Holmes stories, for example, not so much for the mystery problems as for those little glimpses of life and manners in late Victorian England which allow us the pleasure of time travel (without recourse to that curious mechanism invented by Doyle's friend, H. G. Wells). In *Beyond the City,* Doyle is once again a sensitive, faithful chronicler of his era's social habits, intellectual currents, and moral climates. The age comes instantly and vividly to life.

Nor is it true that the novel lacks any matter which might conceivably come under the jurisdiction of the Department of Criminal Investigation. Mrs. Westmacott's treacherous brother, for example, launches a one-man crime wave which begins in embezzlement and ends in assault. Admiral Denver's East End confrontation with Bermondsey Sal and Black Davie is certainly a matter for a police constable (Doyle shows his indebtedness to Dickens in this vignette of London's mean streets). And the crooked partnership of scheming Reuben Metaxa and the dilapidated Dr. Proudie is a foretaste of the white-collar criminal in whom Sherlock Holmes would soon take more than a passing interest.

And then there is Mrs. Westmacott, whose novel this truly is. I envy the reader who is about to make her acquaintance. She is one of the least-known of the great Conan Doyle characters, but put her quaint costume aside and you should have little difficulty recognizing her. The passage of ninety years have failed to make this New Woman old. "She is the type of the woman of the future," an admiring Dr. Walker says, and indeed she is futuristic still. Age cannot wither her charm, nor custom stale the boisterous frankness and resolute fearlessness of her feminism. She is a woman for all seasons.

Doyle's Victorian readers knew all about muscular Christianity. Muscular Femininity was something else again. No doubt Mrs. Westmacott's strenuous athleticism, her weed-puffing and stout-gulping, and her eloquently outspoken opinions struck the genteel reader of 1891 with all the delicacy of a finger in the eye. She is a double-barrelled attack on sexual inequality in the England of Doyle's day and upon the prevalent fictional convention of the Lady. ("Don't, for goodness' sake, begin to be languid and young ladyish!" she admonishes one disciple who has drooped at lawn tennis.)

While Mrs. Westmacott's peculiarities are intended to make us smile, her philosophy is intended to make us think. Beneath the laughter, we can sense a deeper, more sympathetic interest on the author's part with the aspirations (and frustrations) of the late Victorian woman. The vigorous logic of Mrs. Westmacott's impassioned arguments on behalf of women's rights come straight from Doyle's own heart. "No doubt she is a little excessive in her views," as Dr. Walker says, "but in the main I think as she does." So does Dr. Doyle. The nobility and chivalry of Doyle's nature compelled him to take up the defense of woman, play the advocate of her emancipation, and lash out at the hypocrisy of his times:

> "If we are truly courteous, we shall stoop to lift up struggling womanhood when she really needs our help—when it is life and death to her whether she has it or not. And then to cant about it being unwomanly to work in the higher professions. It is womanly enough to starve, but unwomanly to use the brains which God has given them. Is it not a monstrous contention?"

Although Mrs. Westmacott is a feminist of absolute and swift conviction, the majority of her real-life sisters had far more ambivalent feelings about their liberation. On the one hand, they longed to slam behind them the door of the doll's house in which many of them were in fact confined; on the other, they shrank from seeming too assertive, too "unladylike" in pursuit of their goals. Family, society, custom, economic disadvantage, and polite prejudice all conspired to keep them "in their place." For that reason, Doyle's female readers must have found *Beyond the City* a stimulating, even revolutionary, reading experience. Perhaps many of them secretly dreamed of being Mrs. Westmacott. And why not? As a fantasy rôle model, she has everything to offer. She is never anything less than efficient, independent, forthright, and self-sufficient. Though she does not have to work for her living, she has decided to live for her work. She has determined to be admired for her self rather than for her sex. And she will be respected for the success of work performed rather than for the success of dust-free housekeeping, appetizing cooking, or charming hostessing.

Doyle's ardent championship of women's rights is apparent early in the novel. The debate between Mrs. Westmacott and the Admiral in chapter five is a remarkably sympathetic and even passionately eloquent defense of the goals of the women's movement. Does this reflect Doyle's own attitudes? I am inclined to think it does. The heat of the argument is far too intense for this to be merely the stuff of fiction. No one who reads *Beyond the City* can entertain the suspicion that Mrs. Westmacott's eccentricities are really an argument in favour of the *status quo.* We can laugh at her excesses, but we may be sure that Mrs. Westmacott has her creator's full approval when she refuses to immolate herself on the altar of father, husband, and home. "Self-sacrifice is all very well, you know," as she explains, "But we have had rather too much of it on our side, and should like to see a little on the other."

It seems odd to read about sexual equality from Conan Doyle instead of someone like Bernard Shaw, who had gleefully outraged English public opinion by referring to the family dwelling as the woman's workhouse. And yet Doyle can be just as iconoclastic as Shaw. Mrs. Westmacott's initial speeches on the condition of women are as biting and incisive as any Shavian arrows. It is one thing to be revolutionary in a comfortable suburb, however, and quite another to translate social criticism into social action. We have to take Mrs. Westmacott's word for it that the English home can be the nearest thing to a prison for those women sentenced to a life of constant child-bearing and endless household chores. Since the women in this novel move with perfect assurance and freedom, we have to remember that the great majority of women in 1891 had few such assurances and fewer freedoms. Viewed as venerable in the house and vulnerable beyond it, the Victorian woman was seldom credited as a force which might contribute something more to the life of the nation than infants and gossip. Mrs. Westmacott is determined to change all that, and it is obvious that Conan Doyle is squarely on her side. The reader may object that she is really in the wrong place to do her work, but if she is content to preach and proselytize in her limited suburban circle, it may be because she has already exhausted the larger audiences and auditoriums of the city.

Here, then, is Conan Doyle's self-improvement plan for the Victorian woman. She should, he says, attend less to household duties, qualify for some trade or profession, and be allowed free entry into previously closed job markets. The doors of educational and occupational opportunity must not be allowed to slam shut on the qualified female applicant. "Why should the wash-tub, the needle, and the housekeeper's book be eternally theirs? Might they not reach higher, to the consulting-room, to the bench, and even to the pulpit?"

Such enlightened arguments are sure to provoke a nervous reaction on the part of Victorian gentlemen who do not share the author's own powerful sympathies. Admiral Denver, for one, is quick to see where this line of liberal reasoning may lead. He points out that emancipation could result in the rank absurdity of a woman taking command of the Channel Squadron. "Well," Mrs. Denver cunningly replies, "you have a woman on the throne taking command of the whole nation, and everybody is agreed that she does it better than any of the men." I have every confidence that when

Mrs. Westmacott took up her crusade in America, the admiral's wife succeeded her in the chair of the local Emancipation Guild.

Her conservative husband also seems to have enjoyed an afterlife. According to biographer Pierre Nordon, there exists among Conan Doyle's voluminous papers an unpublished play entitled *Admiral Denver.* One likes to think that the play continues the adventures of that doughty old sea dog who survived all the perils of life and war afloat only to have his proud sails peppered by the point-blank broadsides of the Norwood Emancipator.

I have emphasized the theme of female identity as central to the novel, but it is certainly balanced and counterpointed by the theme of male identity. Dr. Walker and Admiral Denver have made great reputations, but they invite two problems by settling in Norwood: loss of the work which has given them personal meaning and loss of control over events which now shape their lives. The doctor loses control of his daughters, who pose as feminists to discourage his interest in that arch-feminist, Mrs. Westmacott. The admiral must journey to London, where he is all at sea among sharks, in a desperate attempt to save his son's imperilled honour. Even strong, simple-minded Charles Westmacott has his crisis, caught as he is between the life of the mind, which his aunt constantly urges on him, and the sporting life at which he is perhaps too proficient. A simple letter of invitation to Ida Walker to go on a bicycle ride can cause him as much pain as the mysteries of Browning, though at least he keeps on hand a copy of *The Secret Solved; or, Letter-writing Made Easy.* Unfortunately, no critic has been invented yet who will explain Browning to him.

The focal point of the masculine dilemma is the rise, fall, and commercial resurrection of Harold Denver. Harold must struggle valiantly to "keep himself free from the sordid aims and base ambitions which drag down the man whose business lies too exclusively in the money market of the vast Babylon." But business also has its attraction, and therein lies unconscious irony. The duty of a man such as Harold is to enter the settled order of a respectable, middle-class life whose measure is successful materialism and whose reward is successful matrimony. It is the inherent condition of this life that the money market will be closely linked to the marriage market, even though Harold avers to his dear Clara that the one has nothing to do with the other. "Here lay happiness and honour, and all that was high and noble; there lay the soul-killing round, the lonely life, the base pursuit of money, the sordid, selfish aims. He needed but the hand of the woman he loved to lead him into the better path."

Harold and Clara can live on love, Harold insists, and maintain a sense of spiritual purity that will help him control the dreaded acquisitive instinct. (From inordinate worship of pounds and pence, and from business partners who abscond in the night, God protect us!) Clara's love will prevent the humanistic Harold from turning into the sort of capitalistic Mr. Hyde which Jeremiah Pearson has already become.

Life in Norwood is as clean and decent as a bicycle ride with a lovely girl in the sunshine of a spring day, but work in London is an ordeal which constantly challenges the moral integrity (as well as the fiscal ingenuity) of the Norwood businessman. Commercial London, as Doyle portrays it, is an amusingly lurid place of money lust and tainted temptation, a place which somehow confirms the secret and sordid criminal nature which lurks in every saintly Dr. Jekyll and noble Harold Denver. "You do not know how degrading this city life is," Harold confesses to Clara, "how debasing, and yet how absorbing. Money for ever clinks in your ear. You can think of nothing else. From the bottom of my heart I hate it."

Yet it is also clear that Harold loves what he hates. He is a good businessman, as well as a good man, and his problem is to keep the one from overwhelming the other. The solution seems simple enough—business and profit in London; love and leisure in Norwood—until we realize that Harold's double life is an evasion of what he fears most in his own nature, the possibility that innocence and corruption may go hand in hand. His anxiety reflects deep-seated Victorian fears about the compromise between necessity and propriety, between selfish instinct and social obligation, between the masterful animal in man and the dutiful angel in him.

Although he hates making money, Harold admits he can think of nothing else. Although he pledges unswerving devotion to his girl and family back in Norwood, the money temples of Babylon-on-Thames snare his secret heart, summon his highest abilities, and test his true worth in a way Norwood never can. Yet Harold insists that London business life is perverse, somehow shameful, even though it is respectable work, work that is part of the accepted social order. To win solid respectability as a city businessman is the dream and envy of every young man who goes to London to seek his fortune, but Harold senses that respectability engenders its own flaw. He reacts by dividing himself into two different people (a comparable case is that of

Wemmick in Dickens's *Great Expectations*), as if to separate out the yang and yin of his own personality. Moneymaking in the city, lovemaking beyond the city, where is the real Harold? Implicit in his confusion is the confusion of Victorian idealism.

So Doyle's simple fable of suburban life reflects the dark complexities of unexamined existence. Some fascinating questions go unanswered. Is "the base pursuit of money" which enriches and enrages Harold really all that different from the pursuit of love? From the pursuit of happiness? From the pursuit of security? If the disease of materialism is so unnatural that only love can cure it, what will happen when the future Mrs. Harold Denver decides that her husband is not earning enough to support her in the style to which she is accustomed? Can our Norwood friends permanently banish the "sordid, selfish aims" which, acknowledged or not, ultimately shape the conduct and govern the lives of men and women everywhere?

On these and other questions, Doyle is wisely silent, as well he should be in a novel of this kind. For all its worldly concerns, *Beyond the City* is only a fairy tale for adults, and a fairy tale must not end in uncertainty or uneasiness. Doyle's novel ends with a round of weddings and the Westmacotts safely relocated on the other side of the Atlantic. Nothing—not even life itself—can intrude on the peace of Norwood now.

It has been said that if, in the course of a novel, the novelist has managed to create just one memorable character whom the reader will recall long after the book itself is forgotten, then his work has not been altogether in vain. Such a character is the justification of the book; he may also be the perpetuation of it, the reason for reviving the novel at a future date and introducing its pleasures to a new generation of readers.

Now that we have this fine new edition of *Beyond the City,* we can see clearly how the storytelling genius of Conan Doyle has given us that character. Surprisingly, it is not the middle-class hero of the Stock Exchange, nor the valiant admiral who vows to return to sea to save his son, nor even the daughter-plagued doctor who can't recognize when his leg is being pulled by household pranksters.

No, when one thinks of this novel, one must always recall the vital, if slightly incredible, figure of the *fin de siècle* feminist. She may be outmaneuvering some hapless male victim, outpointing the pale, prudish Victorian Lady, or merely "bounding into view upon the lawn with brandished racket and short skirts fluttering in the breeze." In whatever guise, she is always ready to wage battle, to win hearts and minds, to score points and advantages for women everywhere. Some readers may find her too hearty, too busy for their tastes. I confess I cannot have enough of her.

Mrs. Westmacott is one of Doyle's most beguiling creations, a staunch soldier in the war against effete sophistication and social stagnation. Had she been brought to the screen as portrayed by a Katharine Hepburn or Diana Rigg, Mrs. Westmacott would surely be a universal household name by now. As it is, she remains that rarest of all fictional types, a comic caricature who is also a "serious" character, a figure of fun who is also a figurehead of a philosophy. In that respect, the eccentric feminist is a companion, a sister, to Sherlock Holmes, the unconventional detective whose merits Conan Doyle could also not resist teasing.

If she is not the most endearing character Doyle ever

created, Mrs. Westmacott is easily one of the most enduring. One wonders how her students at "Emancipation College" reacted to her strange pets and rousing sermons. Perhaps she dazzled the American coeds and inspired them to such lofty feats of assertive behaviour as those which greeted an astounded Dr. Walker one night on his return home:

> The room was full of the blue wreaths of smoke, and the lamp-light shone through the thin haze upon gold-topped bottles, plates, napkins, and a litter of oyster shells and cigaretes. Ida, flushed and excited, was reclining upon the settee, a wine-glass at her elbow, and a cigarette between her fingers, while Charles Westmacott sat beside her, with his arm thrown over the head of the sofa, with the suggestion of a caress. On the other side of the room, Clara was lounging in an arm-chair, with Harold beside her, both smoking and both with wine-glasses beside them. The Doctor stood speechless in the doorway, staring at the Bacchanalian scene.
>
> "Come in, papa! Do!" cried Ida. "Won't you have a glass of champagne?"

So much for Victorian inhibition.

If rum in the morning and champagne in the evening are not enough to send a proper Victorian papa running to the comforts of his club, Ida and Clara contrive their father's total exasperation by taking a consuming interest in *The Lights, Beacons, Buoys, Channels, and Landmarks of Great Britain,* hardly the stuff that dutiful daughters would ordinarily consult in an effort to improve their ladylike characters. Owing more than a little to the high spirits of Doyle's own sisters, Connie and Lottie, the tongue-in-cheek feminism of the Walker girls is the comic apex of the novel. Readers may regret that the mischievous misses capitulate so soon; while their merry pranks last, Doyle's spritely wit is at its most effervescent. Wilde himself might surely have envied that marvelous line in which Ida attempts to stage-manage her sister's appearance of ruin: "Clara, dear, put your feet upon the coal scuttle, and do try to look a little dissipated."

A girl with her feet upon the coal scuttle, her mind in the *Buoys of Britain,* and her head on the shoulder of one of the boys of Norwood was presumably well advanced down the road to perdition. In Norwood, that unpaved road is lined with primroses and periwinkles, as well as feminist intentions.

The reader who enjoys the champagne comedy and sparkling satire of *Beyond the City* should also take note of its value as a social document. It bears witness to a city, a century, and a sex in transition. Eager as you may be to rush off on your sturdy bicycle down these shady, suburban lanes of Norwood, pause a moment. Above the rustle of ivy on brick, the whack of tennis balls, and the chiming of the village churchbell, you may hear the end of an era blowing in the wind.

HOWARD LACHTMAN

March 15, 1981